THIRD

A DC After Dark Novel

ROBIN COVINGTON

THIRD

A DC After Dark Novel

By

Robin Covington

Burning Up the Sheets, LLC

23139 Laurel Way

Hollywood, MD 20636

Visit my website at www.robincovingtonromance.com.

Cover design by: Sweet and Spicy Designs

Ebook ISBN: 978-0-9905432-8-2

Print ISBN: 978-0-9905432-9-9

Manufactured in the United States of America

First Edition May 2017

❀ Created with Vellum

For Stephanie Dray—who told me to write this book at RWA 2015.
Thank you for the encouragement and friendship.

Chapter One

AIDEN

Senator Nathan Marsden was dead and as naked as the day he was born.

I crouched down beside the king-sized bed, pulling on a pair of latex gloves as I took in the all-too-familiar scene before me. Not that I'm used to seeing dead national-level politicians every day. Contrary to the constant parade of thriller movies with dead senators and judges littering the streets, it doesn't happen that often in Washington DC. Street people, junkies, gang bangers, sad domestic cases . . . that's the usual victim I'm called to see in their worst moment and then charged to catch whatever shit bag did them in.

Very rarely was the victim a guy whose face was splashed all over the cover of TIME magazine.

I swore under my breath, already wondering whose karma I pissed on to catch such a high-profile case. I could look forward to everybody in DC with any connection to this case to be up my ass 24/7 until this one closed. Fuck.

The room was very quiet except for the sounds of technical crews doing their part to catch a killer. The air was rank with the odor of death and sex, the vibe in the atmosphere all wrong. Each scene felt off and finding out what caused it was usually the first step to solving the case.

For a dead guy he didn't look too bad. I'd definitely seen worse. His pale body, eyes wide open and covered in the haze of death, was sprawled in the middle of a mess of sheets. Legs splayed wide, his flaccid cock lying against his thigh. He was in shape, a healthy male in his mid-thirties who took care of himself. The bullet hole in his chest and the dark spread of blood under his body were out of place in the upscale surroundings of the hotel room. This was not a by-the-hour joint, catering to the rich and self-important who flocked to DC to broker deals, make money, or fuck somebody over. I wondered which vice lead to the bullet in the chest of the up-and-coming junior Senator from some square state in the middle of the country. I could predict some unhappy Bible-toting constituents who probably weren't going to be okay with why and how this went down.

"What's the estimated time of death?" I asked the M.E. kneeling on the opposite side of the three-billion thread count sheets. I didn't know this one, just one of the new faces in that office that appeared on a semi-regular basis. She was small, with dark hair pulled back into a ponytail, her eyes tired and I wondered how long she'd stick around. The Office of the Medical Examiner was busy and it wasn't the place for everyone.

Just like the Homicide Division wasn't for every cop. No, you had to be my particular brand of crazy asshole to endure year after year of people killing each other and still love the job. And I fucking loved the job.

The M.E. answered without even looking at me, too engrossed in labeling vials and bags and shoving them in her evidence case to give a shit about making eye contact. I was okay with it. It wasn't her job to cater to the living. "Twelve hours or so. Give or take a couple of hours."

"So, midnight or one in the morning," I muttered as I leaned down to get a better look at the body sprawled on the disheveled sheets. I didn't bother to ask what was the cause of death. The bullet hole in middle of his chest was a good indicator of how the Senator had bought it unless the tox screen came back with a surprise. "Must have used a silencer or something for people not to hear. Nobody reported a goddam thing much less a gunshot in the middle of the night."

"And the perp was allowed into the room," Peter, my partner, gestured towards the crime scene techs messing with the front door. "They say there's no evidence of forced entry."

I eased up off the floor, careful not to lean on the bed when my knees and achy joints protested the movement. At thirty-eight I wasn't old and I kept my body in great shape but partying at a bar last night until the wee hours and spending some quality time on my knees servicing the cock of a beautiful boy wasn't conducive to being at the top-of-my-game today. As usual, nothing got past Peter.

"You need help there?" His smirk quickly morphed into a full grin when I flipped him off. A big guy with an imposing frame, his bulk usually made criminals and cops think twice about tangling with him but his smile stripped him of all that edge. It was boyish, bright white teeth against the ebony of his skin and it completely ruined his tough-guy game. "You're getting too old to be running the streets at all hours."

"I was in bed early enough." I didn't elaborate that I hadn't done any actual sleeping in the bed of the man I'd picked up at a club. I didn't need to. We'd been partners long enough for him to jump to all the correct conclusions. I pointed at the body. "So was he from the looks of it."

Several used condoms were in the trash can, their wrap-

pers scattered on the bedside table along with lube and a
large, flesh-colored dildo. That fucker had to be nine inches
long and breathtakingly wide and I mentally saluted the
senator and his mystery sex partner. He hadn't been
conducting constituent town halls in this two-thousand a
night junior suite last night. Not unless he had new and
personal ways of obtaining votes.

The M.E. perked up, sliding a used condom into an
evidence bag. "He had sex. Lots of it according to our prelim-
inary examination of the sheets." She paused as she wrote on
a bag with a black Sharpie. "We'll determine if the semen in
the rubbers is his but there's also evidence of anal penetra-
tion." She pointed her chin at the sex toy lying next to the
telephone. "We'll test the dildo to see if that is what was used
on him or his partner or both. Any DNA we can find we'll
cross-check and get you the results."

I whistled but not in judgment. I couldn't begrudge any
guy indulging in a little ass play if that's what he liked. Hell, I
enjoyed sex with men and women although I'd confined my
activities to the male variety since my divorce. A cheating
wife had soured my appetite for female companionship or any
whiff of commitment for a while. "I wonder what *Mrs.*
Senator Marsden thinks about him meeting up for a little fun
on the side."

"Maybe she was here with him," Peter said, lifting the
edge of the coverlet. His eyes scanned the area, looking for
anything that might be a clue to what had gone down here.
He looked up at me and winked. "You know. Keeping the
spark alive. A little role play to spice things up. Meet in the
bar and pretend to be strangers before heading up to
the room . . ."

I raised an eyebrow at him. "You speaking from experi-
ence? You and Katie . . . " I let my question hang in the air
between us. They were good together, my partner at work

and his partner at home. Solid and still hot for each other even after three kids. They were also the best of friends and it was an amazing thing to watch. I didn't even try to curb my jealousy.

"Fuck off," he chuckled as he reached for something on the floor just under where he was searching. He produced another used condom wrapper and passed it off to the M.E. and her never-ending supply of evidence bags. "*Everybody* knows that hotel sex is hot."

I grunted my agreement, my gaze scouring the scene before me looking for . . . I wasn't quite sure. Not yet. A clue was here and I just needed to figure out what it was. No killer was so good that they didn't leave something behind. The real test was whether the cop was good enough to find the mistake.

"Where is Mrs. Marsden now?" I looked at the uniform cop hovering on the edge of the scene.

He held a cell phone to his ear but placed a beefy paw over the mouthpiece to answer me. "We called all her available numbers but she's not answering. The housekeeper and her personal assistant haven't seen her since last night. We have a couple of officers at the residence and the senator's office now."

I looked at Peter and he raised an eyebrow at me. Eight years of partnership and we didn't need words to make the point: Mrs. Marsden was either victim number two or suspect number one.

She wouldn't be the first wife to off her cheating husband in the hotel room where he was sticking his dick in places it shouldn't be.

I walked around the bed, letting my gaze wander over the upscale furniture in the room. Everything about it screamed "you can't afford this" and I found myself tiptoeing around like a bull who'd just discovered his big ass in a china shop.

There were the leavings of a late-night dinner on the table. Used and dirty plates, an empty bottle of wine and two glasses, one broken and scattered across the carpet.

A dark suit coat tossed over the back of a chair by the window caught my attention. I walked over, picking it up to look it over. Designer label. Senatorial navy blue. Probably cost more than I made in a month. On the low table next to the chair was a clear evidence bag, in it I could see a cell phone, keys, a pack of gum and a business card. I peered over, reading the name on the white and slightly crumpled piece of paper.

"Dr. Carla Androghetti. Doctor of Psychiatry." I looked at Peter. "What's the card of a head shrinker doing in the Senator's pocket?"

I pulled out my cellphone and entered her name into the search engine, clicking on the website when it popped up in the results. I thumbed around until I found a tab labeled "Biography" and I keyed it open. I scanned the information, noting her ivy league education bypassing the rest of the data to zero in on her face. Olive skin, big golden brown eyes and a mouth straight out of most men's wet dreams. I whistled low and flashed the screen in Peter's direction. His eyebrows shot up as he nodded his head in appreciation of the visual.

"She's fucking hot. The kind of woman I'd meet in a hotel and use half a dozen rubbers with," I said, pocketing my phone. "I wonder if she's the one who played 'hide the dildo" with the senator last night?"

"Not a clue," Peter shrugged, tugging off his latex gloves with a loud snap. "But it's as good a place to start as any."

"I'm driving," I said as we both headed to the door. "Driver picks the radio station. I'm not listening to your shit taste in music today."

Chapter Two

CARLA

"Ryker, *please* tell me that's the last appointment for the day."

I looked up as my office manager sauntered into my office. Just under six feet tall, muscular and wiry, his pale skin was covered in tattoos, some of them peeking over the collar and beyond the cuffs of his suit jacket. Starkly handsome, he would be devastating if he only smiled more often. But he didn't and I'd long ago stopped expecting him to. Doing hard time would knock all the smiles out of you and Ryker had known hard time.

"Last one Dr. Androghetti," he replied, placing a stack of paperwork in the middle pocket of my briefcase. We'd been together long enough that he knew I would tackle it all at home after a hot shower or soak and a glass of wine. Like a couple of old married people, we even bickered like one so I couldn't resist reminding him about our agreement.

"If that was the last patient of the day, then you agreed to call me Carla." I shoved away from the desk and leaned back in the leather chair. I gave him a glare but it was half-hearted because today had been a bitch of a day. Helping people was my passion but it was exhausting. "That was the deal once we crossed the boss/employer thing and morphed into friends."

"If I had any clue that the consequence of holding your hair back as you puked in the toilet during that ugly bout of stomach flu would be becoming your BFF, I would have let you drown." His words were harsh but the lift of his lip told me that he wouldn't have *actually* let me die in a bowl of artificially blue water. "It's time for you to get the hell out of here because I have somewhere to be and if I leave you here, you'll work until midnight again."

"Where are you going?" I ignored his crack about my workaholic tendencies, there was no use in denying that this tiger had stripes. But Ryker had let slip that he had plans for the evening and inquiring minds wanted to know. "Do you have a date?"

"I'm going to Landslide." He shrugged at the mention of our favorite club and my excitement dimmed. We went there all the time and it was a great place to hook-up but not for much of anything else. And for Ryker . . . I wanted him to have something besides blowjobs in the back room and one-night stands back at some stranger's apartment. He read my mind because he dismissed it with a slash of his hand. "Don't give me that look. I'm good."

"Will Sebastian be there?"

He shrugged but I didn't miss the tension that settled between his shoulder blades at my mention of the man he wanted but could not have. "I can't afford him so it doesn't matter."

I opened my mouth to start our usual argument, but the appearance of a stranger in the doorway pulled me up short. Tall and leanly built, he reminded me of a mountain with the sharp angles of his face too harsh to make him handsome. Striking. Sexy. Someone you would remember. His gaze swept over me, controlled but interested. Yes, he wanted something from me but his quick inhale of breath told me that it wasn't a professional appointment.

Ryker stepped in front of me, placing his body in between us and I wasn't going to object. I dealt with people with mental health issues all day long and I knew that I could never be too careful. It was one of the reasons I'd hired Ryker, a little muscle in the office never hurt in my line of business.

I stood to greet the stranger just as a larger African-American man filled what was left of my open doorway. His demeanor was more open, inquiring, less intimidating.

The first man was. . .dangerous. Something told me to be careful around him.

"Dr. Androghetti?" He stepped forward, pulling an ID case out of the pocket of his suit jacket. The badge was shiny. It looked real. Ryker took two steps forward and took it from him, scanning it before returning it to him and giving me a nod of confirmation.

"How can I help you?" I ran through my patients in my head. None of them seemed in a place to involve the police.

"I'm Detective Cross and this is Detective Simms. We need to ask you a few questions." He slipped his ID case back into his pocket and my gaze was drawn to his hands. Large with long fingers, scrapes and bruises across the knuckles. Recently inflicted. A man who didn't mind getting his hands dirty. I filed that information away for later.

"Of course. Whatever you need." I took two paces backward, settling when I could lean against the edge of my desk. Ryker moved to the side, standing against the wall of my office. Still close but no longer a wall between us. Detective Simms moved into his orbit, his eyes trained on my watchdog as he pulled out a notebook and pen while Cross crossed into my personal space.

I caught my breath, working hard to slow down the rapid

beat of my heart. To ignore the tightening of my nipples. I couldn't control my reaction to him. I should have been wary, cautious, but I wanted to get closer. To inhale him, to touch him. It was crazy but that explained everything and nothing about sexual attraction. Hormones kicked in and you lost a little bit of your mind. It's what made it so delicious.

"What kind of counseling do you do here, Doctor?" He asked, his eyes trained on my face and completely ignoring the huge diploma displayed on the wall just over my right shoulder.

"I specialize in relationship counseling, veteran counseling, grief counseling, and post-addiction counseling. I help people get through and over some of the hard stuff."

"I see," he said, moving past me to examine my credentials. He glanced down at the top of the credenza, fingers briefly touching the signed baseball from a local Nationals game. "Couples? Kids? Adults?"

"Yes." I glanced at Ryker but he was watching the other guy, laser-focused.

"How long has Senator Nathan Marsden been your patient?" Cross asked, his tone even but there was a subtle change. Something dark coated the edges and all my senses told me to be careful from here on out.

I turned to fully face him and he was looking at me. His face was a void, only his dark eyes betraying his suspicion and controlled violence. Now I knew what made him dangerous, he was a man who chose to keep himself under control because to do otherwise would put him on the other side of that badge. And his control kept him off my couch or the couch of someone like me.

But control could always be broken. You just had to have the right tool.

"Nathan was never my patient, Detective," I said, stepping around the desk to stand in front of him. He was tall, over six feet, but with my heels I could almost look him in the eye. "Are you going to tell me what this is about."

Cross exchanged a look with his partner. It spoke of years together and lots of trust. And something very wrong.

"Senator Marsden is dead. We found him this morning."

I reached behind me, my hand searching for the edge of the desk and the support I needed since my legs no longer worked. Ice cold flashed up my spine and over my skin and bile rose in my throat, my stomach rolling. I felt Ryker beside me, his hand on my shoulder.

Nathan. Dead. I'd just spoken to him a couple of days ago and he'd been alive, excited.

"Was it an accident?" I asked, licking my lips as I sought an answer in Cross' face. I knew it already. "Never mind. If it was an accident you wouldn't be here."

"No. It wasn't an accident," he replied, his expression belligerent. "He was murdered. So, I don't really have any patience with doctor/patient confidentiality, Dr. Androghetti. I need to know why the Senator had your card in his pocket."

"I told you. He was not a patient." I shook my head, sliding a glance towards Ryker. He stared back, his gaze offering no solution other than the truth. "He was. . .Nathan was a sexual partner."

"You were having an affair with him?"

"No." I looked towards Ryker again. This part was always tricky. Rarely did people understand and I didn't feel like I had to justify myself to anyone. But this was Nathan. Dead. Murdered. "No. I had sex with both Nathan and Davina. It's what I do."

"For money?" Detective Simms asked, his voice booming across the office. I turned to face him and his judgment. "Are you a sex worker?"

Ryker stepped towards, everything about his demeanor tight and outraged on my behalf. "Hey."

"No. Not a sex worker. We . . . the Marsden's and myself .
. .we belong to a club. Club D. It's all very consensual and
free-of-charge."

The partners exchanged another one of those looks and I
knew what was coming next.

"Where were you last night?" Cross asked, moving closer
to me. He didn't reach for his handcuffs but the twitch in his
fingers betrayed his trained inclination. My confession had
just pushed me to the top of the people-of-interest list.
"Between the time of ten o'clock and three in the morning."

"I was at home. Alone." I stood, bringing myself to my
full height as I answered the unspoken question in the room.
"For the record, I didn't kill Nathan."

Chapter Three

AIDEN

She was one cool customer.

Dr. Carla Abdroghetti sat across the room, surrounded by four homicide detectives, in a chair specifically designed to guarantee that suspects would confess to anything just to get the hell out of it.

Not her.

She was relaxed, loose and her expression was placid. She had not asked for attorney. She didn't even look annoyed. Most of the suspects in this room fluctuated between scared and anxious to angry and belligerent. Some of them even threw up in the nearby trashcan because their nerves got the better of them.

Not her.

Carla . . . Dr. Androghetti looked . . . gorgeous. Sexy. Tempting. Delicious. I couldn't quite name the thing about her that made my heart race and my blood warm under my skin. It wasn't the dark red dress that hugged her curves or the determined shape of her full mouth. It wasn't the way she casually looked at her watch before slicing my boss with a look that would have had most men cowering behind something thick and sturdy.

No, it was something about *her*. Something that didn't come from clothes or an Ivy-League education or a particular background. You were either born with her type of calm, unshakeable charisma or you would never have it. And fuck me, she had it.

And, fuck me, I would not let it cloud my judgment and keep me from finding out if she'd murdered a U.S. Senator. Because right now she was the number one suspect on a short list of one.

"Gentlemen, I am here by my own agreement and am happy to cooperate with your investigation into Nathan's murder but could we please make it happen soon? I have patients to attend to tomorrow at a very early hour."

Dr. Androghetti's quiet, whisky-laced voice cut through the chatter of the detectives. The bodies around me shifted, all attention on her as she made direct eye contact with each of them. I glanced at my colleagues as they all broke eye contact, looking everywhere but at the woman taking control of the room and the men in it as surely as if she had reached out her red-tipped fingernails and grabbed them all by their collective balls.

She definitely had me by my cock. Damn it. Not good when I might need to arrest her for murder.

"Dr. Androghetti, we appreciate you coming in to talk to us," Captain Smith said, his expression polite but trying to send a clear signal that he was in charge of the proceedings. I thought it was so cute that my boss thought that was actually the case. She was in charge of this show and we all knew it. I might be confused about my attraction to Carla Androghetti but I had no confusion about the fact that she was a dangerous woman. A brilliant and dangerous woman. "We'll try to get you out of here as soon as we can."

"I'm not under arrest and I have a full schedule of patients I need to see tomorrow . . ." She glanced down at her watch and then back up at the Captain and each man in the room. When her eyes locked with mine the sizzle was back, crackling under the skin on the back of my neck and down my spine. I ground my body into the seat, determined not to let her see me sweat. When she spoke, it was like she was talking directly to me. ". . .I'll give you an hour."

The room was silent, not even the sound of breathing breaking the moments as we all processed the verbal grenade tossed into the middle of the room.

The Captain was smooth as glass when he finally responded and threw me on top of the explosive device. "Detective Cross is the lead on this homicide. He'll have you out of here as soon as possible."

All eyes swiveled towards me but I kept my gaze locked on the woman sitting across the room. She stared me down, her eyes wary and cunning. My heart rate kicked up, the sound of its beat heavy in my ears.

Yes, she was a very dangerous woman.

"Dr. Androghetti, can you explain the nature of your relationship with Senator Nathan Marsden?"

"He was a friend. He was also a sexual partner, along with his wife, Davina."

The men around me shifted in their chairs, the scrape of metal legs against the floor and the nervous tap of a pen against a tabletop giving away their reactions. While my men fidgeted and murmured like pubescent boys, she remained calm and composed. The only hint at nerves was the swift lick of her tongue across her lower lip. My own mouth watered at the glistening red left behind, my body ached with a craving to taste her.

"So, you had an affair with the Senator?" I asked.

"No. It wasn't an affair. I was a third in their bed when

they requested it. Sometimes the request came from Davina and sometimes it was Nathan." She moved in her chair, uncrossing and crossing her legs, pulling the eyes of every man in the room to their sexy, toned length and the red pumps on her feet. "We were friends. We were all friends. We met through a club where we are all members."

"Do you often sleep with your friends?"

"I try to make it a point to at least like the people I fuck, Detective," she answered, her lip curling up a little in the corner in a smile. I pressed my own together to stop myself from answering the grin. I should not be enjoying this as much as I was.

"I'll need the name and location of this club." I said and she paused, giving me a cursory nod of agreement but she didn't fill the silence with nervous words or explanation. She waited and I admired her control, her grace under the worst pressure. "Was this an arrangement you had only with the Marsdens?"

"No. I am a third to several couples."

"Is this a regular occurrence then?" I struggled to keep my voice even. The idea of Dr. Androghetti fucking two or more partners of any gender caused my skin to grow tight, my cock to harden slightly in jeans. It was the last place to get hard over a woman but this one had me off-guard, intrigued. I shoved down my thoughts, my physical reaction to her. It was a simple combination of chemistry and timing. Nothing I couldn't handle. "Do you often offer these . . . services?"

She didn't miss the judgment coating my words. I didn't understand what she did. People could do what they liked in the bedroom but sharing wasn't my thing. Not after my divorce. I would never be a participant and I'd never agree to such an arrangement. And if she was mine, I would have never agreed to her playing games like that. It could never end well.

She stared me down, the dark of her pupils taking over the whiskey brown of her eyes as they dilated in anger. Her pulse throbbed under the sleek column of the skin of her neck, her fingers clutching the arms of the chair with almost white-knuckle pressure. She could be rattled. Not to the point of outburst but she had . . . vulnerabilities. It was my job to rip them open and expose them to get the truth.

"Dr. Androghetti, I asked you a question. Do you make it a habit of sleeping with men and their wives? Playing out whatever fantasy they have locked away?"

"It's not always a man and his wife. Sometimes I'm with a man and his husband or a woman and her wife."

"So, you're bisexual?"

She shrugged. "I don't believe in labels. I sleep with who I want, when I want, and on whatever terms I want."

The men around me shifted again, this time their fidgeting augmented by low snorts of laughter. I cut a look at them, intending my glare to shut down their juvenile behavior but once again the good doctor had something to say. I turned just as she leaned forward in her chair and let us all have it. Not that she raised her voice. No, her voice was low and even and not to be ignored.

"You can laugh all you want but let's get something straight. I'm not here to reenact a scene from "Basic Instinct" so I'm not going to cross my legs and give you all a crotch shot to feed your masturbation fantasies for later. I'm a grown woman who likes to sleep with couples. I offer myself as a third because I enjoy it. It's my kink. Everything is consensual and other than giving you this information to find Nathan's killer, I don't have to tell you a goddam thing about my personal life." She eased back in the chair, her posture once again loose and comfortable. "And for the record, I did not kill Nathan Marsden."

I almost believed her. She was dangerous . . . and fucking

magnificent. And I really hoped she was telling the truth because wanting to fuck a murderer wasn't the worst idea I'd ever had but it was pretty damn close.

"Where were you between ten pm and three am?" She'd already answered this once but I wanted to see if she'd slip up with her emotions running high.

"I was at home. Alone."

"Did the Marsden's have a happy marriage?" I threw the question out casually and kept my eyes glued on her. She paused. Not a long stutter, really just a long, slow blink but it was enough to let me know that I'd hit on something potentially important.

"As far as I knew they were happy," she replied, her fingers twisting into the fabric of her skirt for a brief second before she released it. "I just fucked them, Detective. It didn't make us best friends."

I studied her several long moments, contemplating my next move. She wasn't going to fall on the floor and confess and I didn't have enough to run a bluff on her right now. She was confident right now and it was probably a good idea to keep her in that head space. If she was going to make a mistake, Dr. Androghetti would only do it if she felt like she had the upper hand. I'd let her keep that illusion for the time being.

"That's all I have for you right now, Doctor." I stood, offering a smile. Not too flashy or friendly. Just polite and a little bit apologetic. "Please don't leave town without letting us now. I'm sure we'll have follow-up questions."

Peter flashed me a confused glance as he filed out behind the Captain, taking point on the preparations for a press conference scheduled for an hour from now. We had to address the death of the Senator and publicize the search for his missing wife but I had some unfinished business with the witness. The other officers stood up, their chairs scraping against the floor and filling the room with enough noise to mask our continued conversation.

"You don't like what I do," she said, her voice low and even and completely missing any kind of judgment or attitude. She was stating what she'd honestly observed. Straight and to-the-point. I liked that about her.

"It's not my job to like it or not."

"But you don't."

I contemplated her question. What would I gain by answering her? What would I lose by not answering her? Sometimes solving a case was possible because I made a connection with a person of interest who let their guard down and let me in a little too close.

"I don't get it. I don't understand why you want to fuck all these people instead of having a relationship of your own."

"I never said I didn't want a relationship," she stated, her expression sincere but still guarded.

That made me pause. Fuck, this woman kept surprising me and I shouldn't like it but I did. I really wanted to peel back the veneer and figure out what was going on under the expensive Ivy League degree and her designer dress. She was the epitome of "still waters run deep" and I figured that a guy could drown in Carla Androghetti if they weren't careful.

I parsed out my own thoughts, wading through the slog of my own baggage. "That would be . . . difficult. I can't imagine many men . . . or women being excited to know their girlfriend, wife whatever was having a three-way every Wednesday night with you"

"So, you're vanilla," she observed. Not judgmental, just straight forward. I recalled something she'd said earlier.

"I thought you weren't into labels."

The smile was back, just teasing her lips but her eyes were lit up. She was enjoying herself and I was responding, leaning into her space and concentrating on every word and not just because she was involved in my case.

"Sometimes they make conversations easier. Am I wrong?

I huffed out a laugh. I liked her directness. "You aren't right."

Dr. Androghetti stared at me, her head cocked to side as she tried to fit all the pieces in my puzzle. "Fluid? Sexual not gender."

"Open." I wasn't much into labels either but they did make it easier sometimes. I conceded. "Bisexual."

She looked me up and down, her gaze slow and deliberate before she met my eyes again. When she did, my body tightened with awareness. I wasn't the only one feeling this arc between us. She was just the only one who wasn't going to ignore it.

"Good to know," she said.

"Good? For what?"

"For when I'm no longer a murder suspect."

"You're not . . ." I rushed to correct her. I didn't want a high-priced lawyer yelling at me that I'd violated her rights or something.

She waved me off with her hand, her bracelets clinking together with the movement. "Person of interest. Whatever you want to call it."

I decided that it was time to end this line of questioning. I had somehow become as much the subject of our inquiry as she was and that wasn't going to lead to anywhere good for me. Not on a high-profile case.

"As much as I might like how you're thinking, to keep this up could cost me my job. The number one cop rule after "don't shoot your partner" is don't sleep with a person of interest."

She looked at me, the smile back as if she hadn't just

heard me shut this down. "Do you *really* think I murdered Nathan?"

"I think that every person is capable of killing someone given the right motivation and opportunity."

"You're being careful with your words, Detective. You'd make a good psychiatrist."

"Okay, so how careful is this: I think you're a very dangerous woman," I said, letting the challenge coat every syllable. If she wanted to play cat and mouse, I was happy to show her that I still had my claws.

"So, you *do* think I killed him?" She took a step closer and I fought the urge to inch towards her and her heat and sexy invitation. I wasn't a cop because I wanted to play it safe and Dr. Androghetti was the kind of sin I liked to wallow in. Pure and unapologetic. Wild and decadent.

I leaned in closer, whispering in her ear. This close I could smell her perfume, something light and citrus mixed with the warmth of her skin. It reminded me of hot summer days that slid into humid, sticky nights. "That isn't the only kind of danger a beautiful woman brings with her."

She laughed, her breath on my cheek just before I pulled back to look down at her. She had one eyebrow raised and her smile was full this time, white teeth and lush, kissable lips. Lips that would look great wrapped around my dick. Her words pulled me out of the thought of the good doctor on her knees and back to the present.

"I think you're beautiful too, Detective."

"Are you flirting with me?"

"I think we're flirting with each other." She pouted a little, her teasing making me want to sink my teeth into the plump lip. "But that's not allowed is it?"

"No. Not at all." I shook my head, once again having to bite back the smile that teased at my mouth. I enjoyed this woman far too much for my sanity.

I had to remember: she was holding something back and it could be the key to solving this murder. I reached into my pocket and fished out a card, turning it over to write my cell phone number on the back. Holding it out to her I held on longer than necessary when her fingers brushed mine and our eyes locked in desire and challenge.

"This is my number if you decide you want to tell me what you didn't cough up in there" I nodded towards the interrogation room behind us.

"I'm not lying."

I gave her an "A-plus" for the way she lied without batting an eyelash. If I didn't already know the truth, I would have believed her.

"Dr. Androghetti, an omission is the same as a lie when you're dealing with the cops."

She looked down at my card and then back at me before she turned on her high heels and walked away, throwing her last comment at me over her shoulder. "I'll keep that in mind, Detective Cross."

Any good psychiatrist has their own shrink on speed dial.

The man who kept me from curling up into a ball of sniveling goo was an old school head shrinker. He provided a comfortable couch that I wanted to steal every time I stretched out on it and poured out my guts all over his antique Aubusson rug. He answered almost every statement I made with a question for the first thirty minutes and then offered up pearls of wise advice and feedback for the last twenty.

I wouldn't give up my massage time for an extra session with Dr. Stuart Rasmussen but I never missed a session. I couldn't be a good doctor if I didn't.

But when it came down to it and I really needed to talk through what was going on in my head and get it straight, there's a very short list of the people I call. My best friend Jamie was currently in the middle of the move from hell as he switched hockey teams from New Orleans to Washington DC. He's also had his hands full with his new sexy as hell Cajun lover and I never knew if I'd be interrupting something hot and X-rated when I tried to FaceTime.

When Livvy was in town and not jet setting around the world stealing things and screwing her gorgeous husband, she was always good for a heart-to-heart over a bottle of vodka and pedicures. But, according to her latest text they were somewhere over the Atlantic in an airplane and wouldn't be in town until tomorrow.

But my current option wasn't the B-Team. Ryker was a first-rate, gold-medal level friend. He would make a terrible shrink because he never hesitated to tell you exactly what he thought you should do. He didn't give you shit about it if you didn't listen to him but he saw things in a very linear way and he didn't understand why you didn't just walk a straight path between A and B when it was right in front of your face. The only time I'd seen him hesitate was with this little thing he had going with his hot little rent boy, Sebastian. He hadn't asked my opinion on that potentially toxic and destructive non-relationship but I'd be happy to offer it up when he asked.

But he never would.

So this session was all about me.

"What the fuck were you thinking, lying to the cops?" Ryker asked, his anger making his movements abrupt and jagged. He watched his form in the mirror of the gym, only giving me the briefest of hot glares but I got the message loud and clear: he was beyond pissed at me. "Seriously, Doc, what the fuck were you thinking?"

His rage toppled his desire to maintain his ridiculously cut body and he dropped the weights onto the rack, making several people turn and look with the clatter of metal on metal. Reaching over to grab his water bottle, he took a long swallow before he turned to really look at me. One look at his face and I corrected my previous assessment, he wasn't mad. He was scared.

"Doc, you can't lie to the police. They get pissed and put

you in the spotlight and your life is over. Jail would be the least of your worries. You know this. One whiff of your *alternative lifestyle* on social media and you could wave goodbye to at least half of your patients."

The truth of his words made me shift uncomfortably, the heat racing up my skin having nothing to do with our workout. The world of Club D was safe, we worked because everyone had something to lose if our world was exposed. My reliance on the club had made me reckless. I'd been stupid and cocky and left myself open to more trouble than Senator Nathen Marsden was worth.

And I knew why I'd done it. One hot, sexy, broody cop who'd made my thighs clench and my tongue run away with me. I wanted his attention at a visceral level and our verbal sparring had gotten that and more.

"It was that fucking cop," I ground out, plopping my ass down on the weight bench. "He just made me . . ."

"He made you pull out the A-game." He laughed but nothing about it was happy. "I knew the minute you two locked eyes in the office that it was *on*. If you'd met him in Club D, you'd have fucked him before you knew his name."

He wasn't wrong. Aiden Cross had said I was a dangerous woman but he was the one who had "caution" flashing over his head in neon and it was like fucking catnip to me. But I wasn't so sure that he'd ever act on the attraction that existed between us.

"He'd never go for me, Ryker. You should have heard the derision in his voice when I told him about my arrangement with Nathan and Davina. He thinks I'm a deviant and not in the good way."

"But you said he admitted to being bi. He can't get too high on that horse when he likes sucking cock as much as eating pussy," he answered, scanning the room and taking note of each of the patrons. He didn't recognize that he did it anymore but habits developed while learning to survive in prison were not easily broken. "But none of that has anything to do with the fact that you lied to the police in the middle of a murder investigation. The murder of a United States Senator to boot." He shook his head. "Fuck, Doc."

I opened my mouth to argue with him but I shut it. He was right and I knew it. I just didn't like being wrong.

"At the time, I just didn't think that Nathan wanting me to have an affair with him was relevant. He propositioned me once and when I shut him down, he never mentioned it again."

"And you were the only woman he wanted to stick his dick in without his wife there to supervise?" he scoffed, wiping off his forehead with a towel. "You're hot as fuck Doc but I don't think you were the only extracurricular ass he was trying to score."

I thought back to how the last few times I'd been with Nathan and Davina something had felt off-kilter. When you do what I do, all you have to do is watch a couple closely to see when they're not in sync with what is going on. The Marsdens had not been on the same page and it's why I'd backed off meeting up with them recently. I was there to make couples better, closer. Not to assist in their implosion.

As usual Ryker was done with the conversation and he let me know it. I had people on my couch that I couldn't get to shut up and most days I barely got a sentence out of the man before me.

"Call Detective Dickhead and tell him what you know. If you get arrested, I'm not bailing your ass out. I don't go to police stations, they give me a rash."

Chapter Five

AIDEN

"She has a goddam convicted murderer working in her office."

Peter looked at me from across our desks in the bullpen of the precinct. The Homicide Division was on the second floor, a warren of cubicles, old office furniture and Iron Age computers. Phones rang all day while cops worked overtime and families of victims fought to keep our attention and their loved one's case on the top of the ever-growing pile.

It was exhausting and thankless but it was the best goddam job in the world. The son and grandson of a cop, I couldn't imagine doing anything else. And it had saved my sanity in the year since my divorce. It was hard to wallow too long in my shit when a mother mourned the death of her teenage son.

"I presume you're talking about your latest obsession," Peter answered, looking back down at the report splayed across his desk. "Dr. Androghetti didn't kill Senator Marsden."

"I don't think she did either but," I waved the paper I was reading in his general direction. "She has a convicted murderer on her payroll. That guy," I glanced by down at the name entered into the sheet, reading it off, "Michael Dean Ryker was convicted of involuntary manslaughter and did two years in the state penitentiary."

Peter squinted at me, his lips curled in derision. "You don't think *he* killed him do you?"

I hesitated, wishing it was that simple. Everyone wanted a high-profile case until you got one and realized just what a pain in the ass it was to have all the brass, including the fucking mayor of DC, up your ass without lube. A murderer wrapped up in a nice little bow would be amazing right now but it wasn't this Ryker guy.

"No. He has an airtight alibi." I grinned and waggled my eyebrows at my partner. "In fact, he *was* airtight at the time of the murder. Or the hot little twink he fucked with this other guy was airtight . . . I don't know. . . he was in a three-some and they both vouched for him. He was too busy fucking somebody else to fuck the Senator."

"Great," Peter grumbled, his big paw of a hand wrapped around his coffee mug and he took sip. With a grimace, he set the cup down and shoved it away, crinkling papers and burying random post-its in his haste. "So, the only thing we know about Dr. Carla Androghetti is that she has no alibi, slept with both the Senator and his wife, and every time you talk about her, you get a hard on."

I didn't answer him. What was the point? He wasn't wrong.

"What? No denial from you?"

"Would it matter?"

"Nope." He settled back in his chair. The thing was too small for him and every time he moved it screamed for mercy. I was a big guy but Peter was enormous. A football player for the University of Michigan during college, I would have wet myself if he'd come at me during a game. "I know you want to fuck her. I've watched you screw your way through DC for the past year. I know what 'Aiden in heat' looks like. Just don't do it until this case is over."

"I don't think you need to worry about it," I observed, cutting to the salient point on the matter. "She sleeps with couples and the last time I looked, I didn't have one of those." I paused. "Because my wife cheated on me and then left me."

And as if she somehow had a chip planted in my head, my phone lit up and the name of the woman who'd betrayed my trust flashed up on the screen. Her ringtone, a shrill witch's cackle, grabbed Peter's attention and his gaze landed on my phone and then my face as I declined the call and let it go to voicemail. A voicemail I would never listen to.

"She's just going to keep calling if you don't answer her," he said, shaking his head as he looked back down at the paperwork spread out before him.

"Well, my divorce papers pretty much gave me permission to ignore all of her calls."

He grumbled across the desk, mumbling about me and my stubborn stupidity. He didn't want me to get back with Patrice. He'd had front row seats to that three-ring-circus and then watched me burn it down. But he did want me to put it behind me and I hadn't. Not really. I didn't love her, we were over, but I was still holding on to resentment that poisoned me a little each day.

The phone on our desk rang and we both looked at it and then each other.

"I answered it last time," he said, ignoring the shrill ring and my glare. I picked it up, hoping it wasn't a call from the Mayor's office or a reporter.

"Cross," I listened to the beat cop on the other end of the

line, explaining what he'd found. I scribbled down the address and put down the receiver and stood, grabbing my jacket and my cellphone and checking my shoulder holster. Peter glanced up and I smiled. I'd take any break in this case we could get. "They found Davina Marsden and she's alive but the woman with her isn't."

Chapter Six

CARLA

There is nothing more gorgeous than an aroused man stretched out between two women.

Rush, impossibly tall and broad and deliciously sweaty, took up most of the bed in one of the private rooms at Club D. His large frame, covered in tanned skin and dark hair - the right amount in his armpits and across his chest, picking up again just above his belly button and leading down his tight, hard belly in a pleasure trail that ended in a nest surrounding his large, hard cock.

The cock currently sliding in and out of his wife's wet, hungry mouth.

Rush and Livvy were beautiful together. Both fluid and graceful in their movements, every touch was so obviously filled with love and adoration that it made my heartbeat stutter in my chest and my thrusts falter for just a second. She was the light to his dark, the delicate to his rough-hewn granite, her subtlety to his bull-in-a-china-shop directness. His large hands were in her hair, caressing her as the silky tendrils slipped in between his work-roughened fingers. He pressed down on the back of her head, silently encouraging her to take him deeper as I thrust deeper into him, the silicon dildo buried to the hilt in his ass.

He groaned, his hips moving, pressing back into me with every push and I knew he was close. Rush's head pushed back into the tangle of sheets and pillows underneath him, his jaw clenched as he moaned, every muscle in his body taut with the pleasure we were both giving to him. The dark flutter of his eyelashes against his skin was mesmerizing and I could not look away.

"Fuck, yeah," he ground out, his growl causing my own arousal to spike. He was sexy, all-male and unashamed of taking his pleasure in any form and I got off on being the one of the people allowed to give it to him. "Livvy, baby. Love you so goddam much."

His words were let out on a quick breath just before his body bowed with his climax. I kept thrusting, knowing how much he loved to be fucked through his orgasm. Livvy didn't lift her head, taking him deeper and drinking down every drop of his come as her own sweeter groans joined his. I reached out, running my own shaking hands through her hair, tangling my fingers with Rush as he eyed me under lids heavy with satisfaction. I leaned forward and he lifted up, our mouths brushing and tongues tangling in a tender kiss before he fell back against the sheets in a heap of satiated contentment. It was so incredibly sexy and it lit me up, tightening the desire already coiled in my belly.

I gently pulled out of him, unfastening the belt around my waist and letting the harness fall to the floor at my feet in a vibrating tangle of leather and silicon. I missed the tease of the vibrator against my clit as I climbed onto the bed and took Livvy's mouth in a kiss. She tasted of herself and her husband and I dove in deep, taking what she was offering to me, accepting her invitation to stay here in this with them for a little while longer.

Rush joined us, his lips and tongue, the scruff of his beard adding to the need still building between the three of us. Three-way kisses were tricky but we'd been doing this a long time and we had it down. We had *us* down.

We shifted and I ended with my thighs splayed wide over Rush's face, my pussy exposed to his tongue. I groaned when he took the first lick, realizing that I was closer than I realized. My body buzzed with sensation and it spiked even higher when Livvy sucked my right nipple into her mouth. I rode the wave of pleasure for a while, letting the wet tease of Rush's tongue and the sharp pull of her mouth inch me closer and closer to the orgasm I desperately wanted.

I opened my eyes, dropping my head to look down on my friend, her silky blonde fall of hair partially hiding her beautiful face. I lifted my hand, pushing the loose curls back over her shoulder, exposing not only the exquisite sight of her lips suckling at my breast but also Rush, thrusting his fingers in and out of her sex. She rode him with languid movements, taking what she wanted with unabashed enthusiasm.

"Fuck, Livvy," he groaned against my thigh, his breath hot and humid. The briefest nip of his teeth against my sensitive skin had my fingers twisting in the sheets and digging into hard planes of his chest. "You're so goddam wet. Carla gets you so hot. I fucking love it."

I groaned then, grasping Livvy's face and taking her mouth in a ravenous kiss as her husband ate at my pussy and took me to a long, electric orgasm. I moaned into her mouth as the pleasure ripped through me, grinding my pelvis against his tongue, wordlessly begging to him continue as I rode out the last, sweet aftershocks.

Livvy looped her arms around my neck, burying her face into the crook of my shoulder as she came. Her body shook and shuddered, her hips pistoning up and down on her husband's fingers as she bit into the tender skin of my shoul-

der. I laughed, letting the joy of this moment wash over me
and spill over the two of them.

Moments passed and we all fell into a heap of tangled
arms and legs on the bed. Comfortable with each other after
years of friendship with benefits, none of us were in any hurry
to leave. We spent as much time these days drinking in a bar
watching a Nats game as we did getting hot and sweaty
between the sheets. Livvy was one of my oldest friends and
when she'd reunited with Rush, he was added to my selective
roster of people I trusted with my life and my secrets.

"So, your cop is a fucking superstar. His close rate is
almost damn near perfect and the department loves him,
which explains why they overlook it when he bends the rules
sometimes," Rush said, his voice low and gravely in his post-
sex languor.

"He's a dirty cop?" I asked, shifting my head to the left to
look at Rush as he delivered the information I'd requested.
When he wasn't letting me fuck him or vice versa, Rush was a
mercenary and my go-to guy when I needed the real down
and dirty on people. He conducted the security screenings on
the members at Club D and I knew that if there was a closet
hiding skeletons, he would find it.

"No. He's a good cop. Loves the job and wouldn't cut that
kind of corner. He's just reckless, focused to the point of
obsession and walks that line between black and white to get
the job done." He shifted on the bed, his arm wrapping
around Livvy's waist in drawing her close to his side. She
rested her head on his chest, smiling up at me as he continued. "His personal life is fucked up but nothing that hasn't
happened to any other unfortunate bastard a million times
before."

Livvy picked up the narrative in her uppercrust British
accent, her blue eyes sparkling with mischief. "His wife
cheated on him and left him for her personal trainer and

instead of heading to a member of your fine profession he decided to fuck his way through every bar in DC and Baltimore."

"No women," Rush interjected on a yawn. "Just guys. He's avoided the siren call of the evil, deceiving vagina since his divorce."

Livvy smacked at his chest but he caught her hand, covering up his grin with a soft kiss pressed to her fingertips. I watched them for a few moments, enjoying the way they moved together. So different, but perfectly in tune with each other, not only in the bedroom but in every part of their lives. They'd fractured apart once but had found each other again and the bond they had was stronger for the way it had healed.

I wanted that for myself. The eternal optimist and hopeless romantic, I kept searching. No, not hopeless. In the words of Joan Wilder I was a "hopeful romantic". A proud and card-carrying member of that club and I'd ride or die for the man or woman who'd be able to love me without reservation and without conditions.

They were curled together, in that place where you drift between sleep and waking and it was my cue to leave. Our arrangement didn't make me a part of their unit and while I didn't feel like they were excluding me, I knew when the world narrowed down to just the two of them and I was okay with that. Knowing that I'd added to them becoming closer was what kept me doing this.

I slid out of the bed, grabbing my clothes off the floor where they'd been discarded earlier. I slipped into them, doing one last check for stray items when I heard Rush's voice rumble up from the tumble of sheets wrapped around their bodies.

"Ryker's right. You shouldn't have lied to them and this guy's gonna figure it out and when he does, he'll use it. He's smart and a good cop and not a dude you want to piss off."

His grin was loose, only a brief glimpse of white teeth. "He's not like me. I'm a pussycat."

I laughed. Rush was fucking terrifying and he knew it. "More a like a lion, mauling everyone who gets in your way."

"Yeah well, just remember that even kittens have sharp claws."

He meant it as a warning but I smiled. I liked it when my lovers left a mark.

Chapter Seven

AIDEN

Room 215 at the Holiday Inn Express in the middle of nowhere Maryland was a fucking mess.

The beds were disheveled, mattresses half on the floor and sheets tangled and twisted. And in the middle of all of it was the grey, lifeless body of Evie Staller. She was naked, sprawled between the two beds with three bullet holes in her chest. Her eyes were staring at us, already clouded over with the haze of mortality.

I slid on a pair of latex gloves and squatted beside the body, carefully lifting the hair away from her neck to look at the bruises located there. Purple and harsh underneath the skin, they bore the definite marks of a hand. No two. I let the hair fall and examined the rest of her body.

"There was a fight. Her nails are broken. Bruises all over her. Whatever the hell went down here, she was fighting." I glanced over at Peter, his large frame taking up much of the space in the room not occupied by forensic techs and uniformed officers. "What does Mrs. Marsden look like?"

"Like she did that to her," he nodded towards the body on the floor and then glanced around the room again. "The clerk says that Evie checked them in but Mrs. Marsden was with her. He said they looked 'weird' but he's seen weirder."

I huffed out a laugh. "I bet he has."

"Mrs. Marsden is outside in an ambulance. We can talk to her before they take her to the hospital."

"Yeah. Let's do that." I stood and took in the room again. The place was trashed so it was hard to tell what was what but something was off. "This place doesn't feel right, Pete."

"I know what you mean." He motioned towards the door. "Maybe the widow has some answers for us."

We made our way down the hallway, dodging the police personnel occupying every last inch of the space and making enough noise to wake up all the people in the hotel. We called the elevator and stepped inside, taking the two floors down in silence. Peter was chewing on his pen cap which meant he was thinking deep thoughts and I wondered if he was zeroing in on the same thing that was bugging me.

The doors opened and the lobby was quiet with pockets of people standing here and there, whispering to each other as we passed by.

Peter snorted out a low chuckle next to me. "I bet they didn't expect to get a crime scene investigation along with their continental breakfast."

"Don't forget the free newspaper and the indoor pool."

"There's that."

"None of this feels right, Pete." I glanced at him as we walked through the sliding doors at the hotel entrance, the humid air of a summer morning hitting me in the face and raising goosebumps on my arms. "Not a goddam thing."

"No shit."

The ambulance was parked in the circular area right in front of the hotel, surrounded by patrol cars and the medical examiner's van. Uniforms swarmed everywhere, shouting orders and questions at each other as disembodied voices crackled over the comm units strapped to belts and shoulders.

The back doors of the ambulance were wide open and Davina Marsden sat on a stretcher, shoulders draped in a metallic lined blanket with IV tubes coming out of her arm. She was shaking, drinking a cup of coffee with an attentive paramedic hovering close by. Her short, dark hair was a rat's nest all over her head and the tone matched the dark circles under her eyes and the hollows of her cheeks.

When she lifted her head and looked at us all I saw was emptiness and rage. In my job as a homicide detective I'd seen all kinds of people: hurting people, evil people, just plain assholes. Davina was just crazy. I'm sure Dr. Androghetti would have some kind of official medical diagnosis but it would take a blind person to miss the insanity taking up all the space in Davina's mind.

With what I knew about Nathan Marsden, he'd been the typical entitled prick who'd felt it was his God-given right to fuck every woman he'd ever met. He'd also been a big enough dick to not even try to hide it from his wife. If I had to guess, the blankness in her eyes was the result of years of hurt and betrayal and pain.

Not an excuse to murder two people.

But I understood why she did it.

Peter approached her first, his face kinder than mine. She eyed him cautiously, glaring over the rim of the paper cup. "Mrs. Marsden, we've been looking all over for you."

She stared at him, flicking her gaze over to me with obvious distaste.

"Mrs. Marsden," Peter grabbed her attention again, his tone still gentle but more insistent. "Can you tell me what happened here?"

She scoffed, a bark of laughter completely lacking any hint of brightness. "I killed the cheating whore."

Peter and I both looked at each other and then caught the shocked expression of the paramedic. My partner inched forward, close enough to slip one end of the handcuffs over one of her wrists without even batting an eyelash. Davina gasped, her eyes wide and focused on the silver metal hanging from her wrist.

Peter took the open end and closed it over the railing on the stretcher. "This is just what I have to do Mrs. Marsden. You just told me that you killed Evie Staller, so this is what I have to do."

She looked up at him then, her gaze shifting between my face and Pete's, silent tears spilling over onto her cheeks. Her voice was surprisingly clear when spoke, but it was small, almost a whisper. "Am I under arrest?"

"Yes." He nodded, his smile kind but firm. "Yes. You're under arrest for the murder of Evie Staller."

She was silent during the recitation of her Miranda Rights, casually sipping her coffee as the crowd around us churned like white water rapids.

"Do you understand what I've just said to you, Mrs. Marsden?"

"Yes, I understand. I understand." She nodded, her head bobbing up and down and she began a slow rocking back and forth. "I understand."

"We're going to take you to the hospital, Mrs. Marsden. To make sure you're okay and then we'll talk more, okay?" Peter leaned down to try and catch her eye but she kept shaking her head, the rocking increasing as she kept repeating herself over and over.

When she dropped the cup of coffee he jumped back, trying to avoid the spray of hot liquid. The action appeared to snap her to attention and she ceased all movement, all speech as she stared down at the growing puddle at her feet.

Her voice was softer, even and calm but I could hear everything she said even with the noise erupting around us.

"He wanted her. He wanted to be with her more than he wanted to be with me."

"Who? Evie?" I leaned in closer, hoping my question would get her to look at me. "Nathan wanted to be with Evie?"

"Yes," she nodded, lifting her head as the rocking began again, this time accompanied by the rhythmic clang of the handcuffs against the metal railing. "He was fucking her. They met at hotels and in his office. It was against our agreement. We had an agreement."

"So, you killed Evie because she was having an affair with Nathan?"

"Yes."

"Nathan couldn't stay away from the whores. Evie . . . Carla . . ."

That got my attention and I cut a look at Peter who motioned for me to continue. "Carla Androghetti?"

"Yes. He loved fucking her and I got in the way. He wanted her too but she said no. I didn't need to kill her."

"Because she said no?"

"Yes."

"Mrs. Marsden, did you kill your husband?" Peter asked the million dollar question.

She nodded, her eyes cast down at her feet. "I found them at the hotel. Condoms and sex toys everywhere. Nathan naked and laughing at me. Telling me he didn't want me there."

Mrs. Marsden looked at us both then, her face smeared with tears and mascara. She looked sad and hurt and scared and I had an involuntarily quick pang of pity for her. She started crying, huge violent sobs shaking her entire body. "I didn't know there would be so much blood."

The paramedic took over, making soothing noises as she eased her down on the stretcher and strapped her in for transport. Peter and I backed away, closing the doors and giving it two big thumps to let them know that they could take off.

I slid my keys out of pocket and my sunglasses down on my face turning towards the car with a motion for Peter to follow. I walked slowly, my anger gaining steam with every deliberately placed step I took towards our unmarked vehicle. Pete came up beside me and I felt the impact of the look he leveled at me.

I slid behind the wheel and cranked on the engine, my anger causing me to rev it a little bit more than necessary.

"You gonna drop me off at the station first?" He asked, not wasting his time telling me to calm my ass down.

"Yep," I said, turning slightly to back out of the space and the lot. "And then I'm going to Dr. Androghetti's house and ask her why she lied to me."

Chapter Eight

CARLA

"You lied to me, Dr. Androghetti."

I blinked at the angry man standing in the hallway outside my condominium. He was dressed in dark jeans, a white button down dress shirt with his badge hooked on his waistband. I could see the outline of his shoulder holster under his dark jacket, the color matching his current mood.

I peered over his shoulder. "How did you get up here?"

"I flashed my badge to your doorman." He shifted forward into the open space of the doorway, his body language aggressive and confrontational. I fought the urge to take a step towards him and close the distance. He was compelling when he was in my orbit but add on the energy created by his anger and everything in my body responded. Damn it. "Can I come in? We need to talk about your loose understanding of the truth."

I stood to the side, extending my arm in the universal gesture of welcome and closed the door behind him. My condominium was spacious, two bedrooms and baths, large living spaces and an enormous balcony overlooking the glittering DC skyline but Aiden Cross made it feel small. He dominated my space, his granite hardness contrasting with the comfortable lush setting I'd paid a decorator a lot of money to create.

He scanned my home, his eyes taking in all the details and lingering over the personal photographs and details which made this space uniquely mine. It didn't take long but I knew in my gut that he hadn't missed much. Aiden was smart and I knew that he was as good at parsing out what made people tick as I was. Different jobs, different education but we were both experts on piecing together the human puzzle.

He turned to face me and his gaze was full of comprehension, anger, and fear. A shudder ran through me at my own recognition of that emotion. I was also afraid, not of him, but of how he could splay me open and take me apart if I let him. I think I wanted it but I was unconvinced that it was a good idea.

"We found Davina Marsden," Detective Cross said, taking me off-guard with the unexpected turn in our conversation.

Relief hit me and I felt it spread over my skin in a wave of goosebumps. I rubbed my hands over my arms, feeling the silk of my blouse warm with the friction. "I'm so glad. Is she okay?"

"She has minor injuries and was in shock but I think she'll be okay." He watched me closely, clearing weighing what he was going to share with me. "We found her with a woman named Evie Staller in a hotel in the suburbs of Maryland."

"She was with Evie?" I remembered the young woman, a lobbyist in the energy sector. Tall and blonde, she was sharp-eyed and calculating in the best way possible to make it in DC.

"You know her?"

I nodded. "She's a lobbyist and works with Nathan." I hesitated to confess what else I knew about her but his expression told me that he probably already knew it. I scoured my brain for any reason to continue to keep any secrets for Nathan. If Evie was in the middle of this, the gig was up. "She applied for membership at Club D but was turned down because a member objected."

"Let me guess, Senator Marsden?"

"No. Mrs. Marsden. She said that Evie was having an affair with Nathan. She stated that her interactions with her husband had violated their prior agreements and that Evie didn't respect the parameters of their lifestyle. We all voted to reject Evie's application for membership."

"A husband fucking around on his wife with a younger woman? That sounds like a personal problem, not a problem voted on by a board," he said, hands on his hips, displaying his badge and gun in a blatant power play. It was intimidating and sexy and I was distracted by the hardness of his body underneath the material of his shirt and the mouth-watering bulge in his jeans. Detective Cross was all kinds of my catnip and I'd forgotten just how powerful the pull of desire was between us until he'd walked in and invaded my space.

"It is personal until the Club Board recognizes that the proposed member could disrupt the rest of the membership. Our lifestyle is personal choice and involves a commitment between the couple or polyamorous group but the Club is an entity that has to recognize that our entire lifestyle is built on respect and trust. Not all lifestyle clubs function like Club D but it works for us."

"I'm trying to understand where all this respect and trust is when your entire organization is about jumping in and out of people's beds. Doesn't sound like much of a commitment to me," he observed, the edge to his voice reminding me that his anger was just bubbling under the surface.

"It takes a lot of trust and respect to share your body with other people and keep what's sacred protected. Couples who live the lifestyle have to create boundaries and open lines of communication, otherwise jealousy can destroy it all in a minute. That's takes commitment, Detective."

"I need you to finally come clean with me Dr. Androghetti. My death toll on this case is now doubled."

I gaped at him, not really understanding what he meant. "But you said that Davina was fine."

"Evie Staller is dead. Shot by Davina with the gun we think she used to kill Nathan Marsden. Davina kidnapped Evie and killed her early this morning." He reached in his back pocket and pulled out his handcuffs. I took a step back and he advanced on me. "So why don't you stop lying to me or keeping whatever secret you're keeping before I arrest you for interfering with a police investigation."

I eyed the cold silver object in his hand, the metallic clank of the cuffs reverberating in my body as a delicious shiver of anticipation. I licked my lips and his fingers clenched around them. He made a sound, something low and guttural, living somewhere between a growl and groan of pain. I snapped my gaze to his and the anger-laced need in them made me retreat. He advanced on me and I stumbled back, my legs bumping into the arm chair I'd placed next to the front entrance.

Detective Cross invaded my personal space, his body heat radiating his anger and frustration and lust. I leaned into him, my body ignoring the signals in my brain which tried to pene-trate the desire-haze and get me away from this man. He was everything I wanted and nothing that would be good for me. Our bodies connected, my hardened nipples brushing against his chest with every one of my rapid exhales. Aiden leaned down, his face close to mine, our breaths mingling intimately.

He groaned, his eyes shutting for the briefest moment before they flashed open, the blue almost obliterated by their dilation. His brows furrowed for a split second betraying the last vestige of his indecision.

"Oh, fuck this," he said, reaching out with one hand to spin me around. Before I knew it both of my arms were captured behind my back and the cold metal of the handcuffs tightened around my wrists. The final snap of the lock excited me and I whimpered, a visceral involuntary reaction to his power over me. "Maybe you need an incentive to stop jerking me around?" He pulled on the cuffs, bringing me back into contact with the hard length of his body. "Last chance before I take you down to the station." Another tug on the cuffs and I pushed my ass back against him, causing his next question to stutter. "What didn't you tell me?"

His breath was hot on my neck, his lips brushing against my earlobe and I had to force myself to concentrate on the question.

"Nathan approached me outside of the third agreement I had with him and Davina. He wanted to have an affair and I said no." I swallowed hard, trying not to press back against him but I tugged on the cuffs enough to feel their confinement. I took a steadying breath but I couldn't erase the gravel that scratched at every word. "I said no and then I terminated our third agreement."

He cursed and spun me around, not letting go of my wrists. In this position, we were pressed together from chest to thigh and neither one of us struggled to increase the distance between us. I looked up at him, my heels closing the gap between us but he was still taller, a towering bulk of muscle and man taking up all the available space.

"So, Senator Marsden wanted to fuck you? He wanted you all to himself?" He examined my face, the wicked grin tugging at his mouth incongruous with the unleashed anger that made his muscles tremor. "I don't blame him. I don't like to share either." He leaned in even closer and this time his words were spoken against my lips, each syllable laced with the sharp tang of forbidden lust. "I knew you were lying to me and I still wanted you."

"And you don't want me anymore?' The words were sliding over my tongue before my brain could censor. Laced with honeyed seduction, they were calculated to make something happen here that I didn't know if either of us was ready for.

"I shouldn't."

I recalled what he'd said the first time we'd met. "Because I'm a dangerous woman."

"Fuck yeah, you are," Aiden leaned down closer, his lips brushing over mine before he pulled back slightly. "I'm going to do something really stupid here. Speak now if you don't want my hands all over you."

I stared at him, taking a moment to weigh my options but there was really only one choice. I tugged at the cuffs. "Leave these on."

"Goddam," he huffed out on the last breath before his mouth covered mine.

His kiss was not gentle and he was in total control. Aiden kept a tight hold on the handcuffs, keeping my arms pulled taut behind me and my body wedged between his body and the chair. I leaned into the connection, trying to take my own turn at dominance but he was having none of it.

He tasted of coffee and mint and a musky maleness that made me chase his lips every time he pulled away to take a breath or adjust the angle. I couldn't do much more than open to him, arching into his touch, urging him with my movements to fulfil his promise and put his hands on me. Aiden pulled back and laughed, dark and rough with his own power.

"You want something?" I glared up at him, a move that only made his lips twist in a smile that only be described as devilishly evil. I shivered with almost giddy anticipation. This guy was so bad for me and I loved it. "You want me to touch you, Doc? Here?" His rough fingers grazed the skin on my neck, tracing a path down to my collarbone, lingering over the "V" of my blouse. "Here? That feels good, right?"

"It could feel better, you bastard," I gritted out.

"I think you need to tell me what you want, Doc. I don't have special head-shrinking powers like you do."

"Fuck you." His attitude was pissing me off and making me hotter for him. That pissed me off even more.

"I'd love to fuck you, Doc. Bury my dick so deep in your pussy and keep you wet all night long." He ran a fingertip along the edge of blouse, dipping in to tease the curve of my breast. I whimpered and pressed my body against his touch. "But you've got to use your words first."

I gave in on a growl. "I want you to touch my breast, pinch my nipple. Suck on it. Bite it." I licked my lips. "Do it now."

"Next time I'll make you ask nicely," he said before he released the top two buttons on my blouse and roughly shoved my bra to the side.

The colder air of the room hit my flesh for the briefest second before his mouth was on my nipple and all there was was wet and heat and the rough velvet of his tongue.

"Jesus," I moaned, thrusting myself deeper into his mouth as he sucked in a slow and steady rhythm. My breasts were sensitive, his attention increasing the wetness slicking my thighs under my skirt. I squeezed my legs together, trying to create some friction to get me off.

Because I really fucking needed to get off. Detective Cross had wound me up since the moment I'd met him and this was just the culmination of a week of foreplay.

He pulled off my tit with a pop and looked up at me from under the fringe of dark lashes. His cheeks were ruddy with arousal underneath his stubble, lips swollen with our kisses but it was his smile that took my already ragged breath.

"Get on your knees, Doc."

———

AIDEN

I reached for my belt, unbuckling it as I watched her process my demand.

I undid the button and lowered the zipper, tracking her eyes as they dropped to my crotch. I stopped my progress, reaching out to put a finger under chin to make her look at me.

"If you want my cock, you need to get on your knees."

She stared at me and I counted the seconds, hoping that I hadn't pushed her too far. Carla Androghetti pushed every fucking button I had and this was not where I'd expected this go. I'd come to her apartment, half determined to arrest her and now all I could think about was having her mouth, or any part of her, on my dick.

I let out a long breath of relief when she eased down, astoundingly beautiful and graceful as she executed the move in the incredibly expensive fuck-me heels she was wearing. Her right breast was still bared to me, wet with my saliva and I rolled the taste of her over my tongue. She settled herself on the floor, pausing for a moment before she squared her shoulders and raised her head to look me in the eye.

Breathtaking. Mesmerizing. Way-out-of-my-league-fuck-ing-beautiful. Dark eyes, golden skin, curves everywhere. Jesus, she made me hurt all over.

I hooked my thumbs in the waistband of my jeans and my underwear, pulling them both down to expose my cock. Carla dropped her eyes again, licking her lips at the sight of my penis and I groaned, grabbing myself in a firm grip and pumping it slowly. I reached out with my free hand, tipping her face back up again to make her look at me.

"I want you to suck me. I'm gonna fuck your mouth so good." I shifted forward, teasing her lips with the tip of my cock.

She opened, her tongue reaching out to swipe at the head. I needed no further invitation. I slid my length inside, gritting my teeth at the wet, slippery heat inside. I withdrew, easing back inside she dropped her jaw, opening wider for me and dropping her head back slightly to allow me easier entrance.

"Fuck. So sweet," I groaned, mesmerized at the sight of my cock, slick with her spit and glistening in the light from the nearby lamp before it disappeared inside her heat. Carla moaned, my balls tightened at the sound that vibrated around my length. "Yes. Take it."

I slid my hand around her neck, holding her in place as I thrust my hips forward, enjoying the feel of the suction as she drew me inside. My dick slid in deeper and she choked a little and I pulled out, running my fingertips across her hair in a soothing caress. Carla's eyes opened to gaze up at me, dark eyes shimmering with the unshed tears of lust and surrender.

"Why did you lie to me? Were you afraid to tell tales on your lover?" She shook her head in denial and I ran a finger down her cheek, ending at the side of her mouth, stretched around me. I pulled out, grazing her swollen lips with the head, asking the question I needed to have answered more than anything. Beyond my own understanding of why I needed to know. "Did you love him? Nathan?"

Her answer was fast but not rushed, voice hoarse from our sex. "No. I just fucked him."

"That's cold."

"It didn't mean I didn't care about him. I liked him

enough to let him touch me. It's not something I offer up to just anyone." She tilted her head up in a gesture of pride and defiance. Even on her knees, she would not demean herself in ways that truly mattered. I liked that about her. I didn't understand her or her lifestyle but I respected her unapologetic defense of it.

"So, lucky me," I drawled, dragging my thumb along her bottom lip.

"You have no idea," she said before she leaned forward and swallowed me down to the root.

I gasped, my hips thrusting forward involuntarily as I raced for the pleasure she promised with her lips and teeth and tongue. She kept her eyes on me, sucking me with a sweet, dirty enjoyment that had my orgasm sparking to life in the base of spine. Three more thrusts and it raced through me and I shot into her mouth, down her throat as I grasped her face with both my hands and used her.

Stars behind my eyes, lightning in my blood. Fucking heaven.

Carla moaned, struggling against the cuffs, the metallic clank of the restraints mixing with my groans and her gasps for breath. I pulled out of her, yanking her to her feet and taking her mouth in a kiss filled with more brutality than finesse. Tasting of her unique sweetness and my own come was pure sin and darkness.

She made me crazy, this entire scene feeding the insanity of desire I'd developed for her since the moment I'd laid eyes on her. Arrogant and self-possessed, it made no sense but I'd been determined to have her since I'd learned that she shared her body in a way that defied conventional commitment or relationship.

The thought that she had been and would be on her knees with anyone else made me irrationally possessive.

Releasing her from my kiss, I moved behind her, grasping

the cuffs in my hand to maneuver her towards the back of her couch. I bent her at the waist over the back, spreading her legs apart as I dropped to my knees behind her. I lifted my hands, shaky as they were and dragged her skirt up and over her ass, removing her panties to expose her sex to me.

"Aiden, please," she begged and I wasted no time in giving her what she craved and what I fucking thirsted for.

I spread her cheeks, burying my face in her pussy and eating her out with ruthless determination. I wanted her to come, I wanted to feel her come apart and know that I did that to her and I'd fool myself into thinking that it was the best orgasm she'd ever had. Why I felt the need to fight the shadows of her other bed partners was a thought I chased away by sucking her clit and sliding two fingers into her pussy.

Carla writhed against the couch and then back against my face and I groaned, slapping her ass with my free hand.

"Be still or I'll stop," I nipped at her rounded ass, liking the reddened mark that I knew would be there tomorrow. "Don't move and I'll get you off."

"Make me come you bastard. Stop teasing," she growled over her shoulder, her eyes flashing through the fall of hair partially obscuring her face.

"Like I said, next time you'll ask nicely," I said before I lowered my head and ate at her clit, licking and sucking her pussy as her thighs trembled with her effort to remain still and follow my directions.

I rewarded her by keeping up the tempo, wetting my thumb in the slickness of her slit and rubbing into the rim of her anus. Carla cried out and I pushed in, breaching her hole up to my knuckle and she came. She ground her pussy against my face, her breathing reduced to pants punctuated by a verbal torrent of filthy nonsense.

I rose to my feet, draping my body over hers where she

rested against the couch. She pushed back against me and my half-hard cock rubbed against the wet softness of her sex. I leaned forward, burying my face in the sweet spot of her shoulder, inhaling the lemon scent of her hair while enjoying the silk of it against my face. Her breathing slowed along with mine and we floated in the silence of the room. Lust and anger disappeared with the softening of my penis and the cooling of the sweat on our skin. The impact of what I'd done hit me right between the eyes.

I was a cop. She was . . . I wasn't sure what she was to the case anymore but this was not how I was supposed to use my badge.

"Fuck," I whispered my regret against her skin and she stiffened underneath me. She tried to buck me off, trying to squirm out from underneath me. I pressed down to subdue her, to control her movements but she increased the strength powering her movements. I lifted up as she stood, glaring at me over her shoulder.

"Take these fucking cuffs off me." Carla shoved her hands towards me.. "Now, dammit."

I hefted my jeans up and reached inside my pocket for the keys. I unlocked the handcuffs barely having time to slide them off her wrists before she wrenched away and rubbed the red marks left on her skin and yanked down her skirt. I watched her warily, re-fastening my jeans and belt before taking a step towards her.

She stood her ground and one of her hands whipped out in front in the universal signal for "don't even fucking think about it".

"Carla . . . Doc . . . I'm"

"If you fucking say you're sorry I will slap you," she thrust her head towards the door. "Don't ruin my post-come bliss by being a fucking coward. You wanted it and you took it. Get out."

I stared at her, feeling like multiple levels of some kind of shithead. I couldn't tell if she was pissed because she also regretted what had just gone down or she was pissed at my reaction. Either way, she wasn't going to let me hang around to find out.

When she turned her back on me I had some kind of answer. I walked out the door, closing it firmly behind me.

Chapter Nine

AIDEN

Peter lived in one of those picture perfect houses in a picture perfect neighborhood.

His wife Katie and their two kids weren't perfect but they loved him and he adored them. They argued and loved and supported and kept each other accountable. Their house was a refuge, a place where they could find peace and acceptance and they'd opened their home to me more times than I could count. When my marriage had blown apart, they'd taken my drunken ass in and let me sleep it off in their basement. Katie had organized the packing up of my stuff out of my house and Peter had helped me move it into my new apartment.

I'd kept them in the divorce and I knew how lucky I was.

So, the last thing I really wanted to do was tell Peter just how royally I'd fucked up. But here I was sitting in my car in front of their house trying to put my balls back on and go inside. My phone rang and I jumped, looking down to see Peter's face on the screen. It was a shot from one of the many times I'd sat on his back deck, drinking beers and making him laugh. At me . . . not with me.

"Yeah?" I asked when I answered the call and his voice filled the space of my car.

"Katie says you have to get your ass in here before the neighbors call the police. She says that you are the quintessential definition of 'suspicious'".

"I . . . I fucked up Pete." It was all I could think of to say and the silence that followed didn't bode well for this conversation.

"I'll be out there in a second," he said and the call disconnected. I stared out the front windshield, nodding at the man walking his teacup fluffy dog and looking like he was going to dial "9-1-1" any minute. He hurried away as Peter opened the door to my car, tossing out a "say hi to Evelyn for me" before he lowered his huge bulk into the passenger seat of my car. He smelled like grilled hamburgers and he was wearing an apron which read, "You can't scare me. I have two daughters."

"I'm glad to see you like my gift," I said, gesturing towards him. "Told you you'd wear it."

"Katie says I have five minutes or she's going to make me eat a veggie burger. I'm not eating that shit for anybody so tell me what you did."

"I went over to Dr. Androghetti's house."

"I figured."

"It didn't go as planned."

"Oh, Jesus," Peter hit the dashboard with his hand and I jumped. He was already pissed and he didn't even know what I'd done. "Did you fuck her?"

Okay, maybe he did.

"Yeah. I mean I didn't *fuck* her . . ."

"Did any part of your dick enter any part of Dr. Androghetti's body?" Peter was staring me down across the center console, his anger rolling off him in waves of disappointment. "Did it?" He didn't stop long enough for me to answer. "Of course it did because you were eye-fucking her the every time you got near her."

"I know I fucked up," I rubbed my hand across my jaw and looked outside the window at the suburban perfection laid out in half-acre lots and split-level dream homes. "I'll be lucky if she doesn't make a complaint to the Captain."

"Aiden, you've got to apologize. Make it right. I don't want to break in another partner."

I turned my head, glaring at him across the car. "Nice to make it about you, asshole."

"I'm not the one who fucked a witness or whatever she is at this point." He reached for the door and then paused. "Did you at least find out what she was lying to us about? Please tell me you did your goddam job before you got your dick wet?"

The way he said it just raked across my nerves and I couldn't hide my irritation. "Don't talk about her like that."

Shit. I sounded like a middle schooler and Peter was giving me the side eye from his seat.

"Don't tell me you're into this woman." He gave me a hard look, dead in the eye. "She sleeps with all kinds people. Couples. Threesomes. Whatever else they get up to at Club D." He shoved at my chest, his large paw of a hand pushing my back against my door. "She was screwing the murder victim in our case *and his wife*. You do remember that, don't you?"

"I remember." I sighed and leaned my head back on my seat, staring up at the ceiling. "Marsden asked her to have an affair with him. Just him. Outside of the third arrangement they had with his wife."

"And the Good Doctor said?"

"No." I looked over at him. "She said no and stopped seeing them."

A few moments passed before he answered. "Yeah. She

would." He laughed to himself as he reached for the door, opening it a fraction of an inch, the cool breeze of the evening rushing into the car and bringing with it the scent of grilling meat. I glanced at the clock and noted that ten minutes had passed. So, it was likely grilled veggie something. Poor Pete. "You know she's completely out of your league."

"Yeah. I do."

"She's going to eat you alive. You're going to crash and burn with this woman."

"Uh huh. I know."

"Good" He thunked me on the chest again before fully opening the door. "Technically she's not a person of interest or a suspect in our case anymore so you should be okay unless she makes a complaint to the Captain that you handcuffed her and threatened to arrest her."

I just stared at him. How was I supposed to answer that?

He rolled his eyes and heaved out of my car. "Just fucking fix it Aiden. Apologize and make it right."

I watched my kids glide across the water in the scull.

They were flawless. Not that they didn't make mistakes. No, they needed more practice to become a single, solid unit of muscle and brains but they had come so far. Poor kids from broken homes and at-risk they were learning teamwork and dedication and commitment out on the water and I couldn't have been prouder.

"They look good," Tyrique slid up beside me, his voice deep but tinged with a little bit of teenage wobbliness. At sixteen he was already towering over me, his body strong and his heart even stronger. He was a good kid and I loved that he was taking such a leadership role at the center and here at the rowing club. We weren't supposed to play favorites but I did when it came to him.

"Yeah. They do, "I agreed, sliding a glance over to him, pleased to see the self-satisfied grin on his face. I nudged him with my elbow, making him laugh. "You've got a lot to be proud of here."

"Nah, it's all you Doc." He waved me off, turning back

towards the boathouse, his progress abruptly stalled out by something behind us. "Hey. You need something?"

I turned to see who was he was talking to and stopped mid-turn. Aiden Cross. Looking contrite and sullen and entirely fuckable on my pier. I wanted to kiss him and punch him at the same time. Not a good mix of emotional reactions for someone trained to parse out other people's emotions.

"I'm here to talk to Carla," he answered, moving towards me but stopping when Tyrique edged partially in front of me, his body language saying loud and clear that Aiden was only getting near me if it was through him. Aiden paused, his gaze taking in the long form of this man-child acting as my protector. "It's okay man. I'm a Police Detective."

Tyrique scoffed, his distaste evident in the sound and his body language. "No offense but being part of the 5-0 doesn't exactly put you at the top of my 'trustworthy' list."

"It's fine, Tyrique. He's fine," I placed my hand on his arm and gave him a smile that I hoped translated as the truth. Yeah, I had a problem with Aiden but it wasn't because he was a cop and I didn't want to reinforce Tyrique's already skewed perception of law enforcement. "I know him. This visit is . . . personal."

Tyrique looked between us, his eyes narrowed with his suspicion. He was my protector, my knight and I worried about him taking on the role for yet another person in his life. With a mother working two jobs, Tyrique already looked after his younger brother and the kids at the center. He didn't need to add me to the list as well.

"Is he the reason you've been upset?" Tyrique pointed at him and I reached up, wrapping my fingers around his wrist to lower his arm. I turned him towards the water, gesturing towards the kids in the scull. I ignored his question.

"You make sure they get in safely. Okay?" I looked up at

him, smiling back at him when he gave me a tentative one. "Thank you. We'll be in the boathouse office."

I turned, motioning for Aiden to follow me, pausing briefly to adjust a container of life jackets sitting next to the door. I needed to remind the kids to put that away before they left to head back to the center. We were expecting rain and it would suck to let the jackets get waterlogged and moldy.

I opened the door to my small office and ushered him in, going out of my way not to brush against him as he maneuvered his large body through the opening. His scent, masculine and sharp, filled the space when I closed the door and I remembered how it had lingered on my skin after he'd left me last night. I'd debated showering, opting instead to go to bed with him all over me. I'd woken aching and wet, pissed off and embarrassed.

And now he was here and I was having a hard time maintaining a certain level of anger when I also wanted him. Badly.

"So, you work with these kids? You teach them rowing?" We both looked out of the window, the scull flashing across the horizon as the teens worked together as a team.

"I volunteer at the Anacostia Youth Center. I started offering free counseling to the kids there, especially the LGBTQ kids, and then it expanded to my starting the rowing program. I rowed in college . . ." I let my train of thought lapse, feeling suddenly like I was babbling to fill the space. It wasn't like me. Another testament to how much Aiden threw me off balance.

"Georgetown. You were very good." Aiden gave me a tight smile at my surprise. "I did a background check on you. It was standard protocol."

"For a murder suspect. Yes. I understand," I said as I moved away from him, leaning against the desk to get this thing started and ended. "Why are you here, Detective? Coming to arrest me after all?"

He flinched, the quick recoil of his body at my words told me that they had hit the mark I intended. Whatever he was here to do, I wasn't going to let him off easy.

"No." He cleared his throat, stepping in closer to me, hand outstretched. Now it was my turn to shift back, as much as I could retreat from his touch with the desk behind me. "I came to apologize. I'm sorry" I opened my mouth to warn him off apologizing for what had happened between us. That I couldn't stand. His expression twisted into a knot of anger and resolution. "I'm not sorry that I touched you. Fuck, I've wanted to do that since I first laid eyes on you. I'm sorry for using my badge. That was wrong."

I knew he wasn't lying to me about this. I don't know how I knew but I chalked it up to years of training on reading people and parsing out whether the things they said matched what they were really feeling. Aiden Cross was not a liar. That much I knew of him.

"Fine. Apology accepted," I said, moving to open the door and show him out. I sounded prim and cold and that is how I needed it to be to get him to go. This was never going anywhere between us and I didn't want to show my hand or my heart. "The kids will be back soon. I need to get out there."

I was shoved against the door, his body crowding mine with all his heat and muscle. I should have grabbed the door but my arms twisted around his body, my fingers curled into the fabric of jeans, holding him close to me. It was involuntary but exactly what I wanted and now he knew.

His breath was hot on my cheek as he spoke, his fingers rough in my hair and down my bare arms. His skin was calloused and I shivered at the sensation of his touch.

"I'm not sorry that I tasted you. I'm not sorry that I will never forget what it looked like to have you on your knees with my cock in your mouth." His finger trailed across my cheek, ending in a sensuous swipe against my lower lip. I opened on a gasp and he slid the tip in a little bit, teasing the sensitive space just inside. My belly grew tight and my thighs clenched. "I'm not sorry that you came all over my mouth. I want it again."

"Aiden," I breathed out on a moan and then a gasp of surprise when he spun me around.

"Say it again," he demanded.

I swallowed hard, willing my voice to actually work under the weight of his desire and my own. "Aiden."

His mouth was hard on mine, tongue deliciously intrusive as I opened to him.

I met him wet thrust for slick slide, my fingers digging into his hair to pull him down to me. He groaned and I shifted beneath him, opening my legs wide to allow him to wedge his body between them. His cock was hard underneath his jeans and he ground it against me. It wasn't the right angle so I lifted my legs and wrapped them around his waist, leveraging off the door to hump him.

It wasn't elegant. It wasn't sophisticated. It had all the earmarks of a teenage grope fest in the back seat of my parent's car except now I knew how good sex could be and how to get it. I knew Aiden could give it to me.

And fuck me. I wanted it. Wanted him.

"Hey Doctor Carla!"

The sound of J.J. yelling for me from the pier just outside the very open window of my office quickly ripped me out of the family station wagon and back to the present where I had responsibilities. And the first one was to avoid being caught having sex by these kids.

"Stop. Stop," I said, breaking the kiss and lowering my feet to the ground. Aiden chased my lips, his hands cupping my face to hold me in place. I reached up, tracing his eyebrow before moving upward to grab his hair and tug him back. "The kids are back. Stop."

"Shit," he said, banging his palm against the door in his frustration. He dropped his forehead against my own, his breath harsh against my face. "Shit. Fuck. Shit." He opened his eyes and met my own, using the weight of his body to keep me where I was. "I've got to see you again."

"Bad idea." Such a colossally bad idea. I was who I was and he was who he was and what we wanted didn't match. Not one little bit.

"Wrong answer." He pressed his lips against mine briefly, his tongue sweeping inside for less than the length of a heartbeat. "Go out with me."

"What? On a date?"

"Yes. A date."

"Like dinner and a movie?"

He tilted his head, smiling down at me with wicked allure. "I was thinking of cold beer, hot dogs and a Nats game. I remember that you like them." My mouth fell open in shock and he lifted his hand and shut it slowly, his grin all kinds of cocky now. He ground his groin against me and I sucked in a breath, my eyes half-shuttering with the jump of my own arousal. "And then I want to fuck you."

I stared at him, drawing my lip between my teeth, knowing that this was the edge of the cliff and I had no way of knowing if there were rocks below. All I knew is that I wanted him and he knew me, knew about my kink and still wanted to see me.

No wondering how long before I told him. No awkward conversations explaining about Club D. No seeing them pull away and disappear with empty promises to call once their work wasn't so busy. He knew it all already.

Maybe I could take a chance.

I smiled at him. "You had me at hot dog."

Chapter Eleven

CARLA

Aiden's apartment overlooked the ball park.

Surrounded by new condominiums and almost-high-rises, his building was old school with a dodgy elevator that slowly took me to the sixth floor. It wasn't glamorous or new but it was clean with high ceilings and huge trim along the ceiling. I walked down the somewhat gloomy corridor to 6C and knocked, listening as his footsteps came nearer and nearer. I sucked in a breath and once again asked myself what the fuck I was doing here.

He opened the door and I remembered why I was there. He was so sexy in old jeans and a faded Red Hot Chili Peppers t-shirt. He grabbed for me, his fingers closing around my wrist and dragging me inside.

Aiden's fingers were buried in my hair, his grip holding me still as he kissed me. It was hungry and wet and I looped my own fingers into his waistband, loving the feel of his heated skin against my own. He moved backwards, ramming me against the wall with his body and trapping me there with his heated bulk while I struggled. Not trying to get away but to get closer, clothes-off-him-buried-deep-inside-me closer.

Suddenly Aiden pulled back, breaking off the kiss. He stared down at me, smiling and shaking his head as if to clear it of the fog of lust enveloping us.

"I didn't think you'd actually come."

"Aiden," I gasped, stuttering in and out with my ragged breaths and I tried to bring him back against me. I could feel the chill of the loss of his body heat and I missed him.

"I like it when you call me Aiden." He kissed me hard and fast. "Too much. Fuck."

He clasped my hand, pulling me through his apartment towards two large glass-paned doors leading to a huge open patio. I tugged back at him, urging him to slow down so that I could take a look at where he lived. It was small, one bedroom visible through an open door off the living area. An exposed brick wall with a large flat screen mounted on it and comfortable leather sofas covered in a deep brown angled to create a seating area in the midst of the hardwood floors. The kitchen was marked off by an island, four barstools pulled up for seating.

I liked it. It was warm and lived-in and no-nonsense like the guy standing next to me.

"It's not much inside but I chose it for the view," he said, resuming his leading me out through the double doors and outside. The night was balmy, summer heat and humidity enveloping me as soon as I stepped out but I didn't notice. He was right. The view was fucking awesome.

"Are you kidding me?" I asked, rushing to the edge of the patio to look over a block and a half and right into the ball-field at Nationals Park. The lights were on, casting a harsh white glow on everything around it. We'd need binoculars to see everything on the field in detail but you could hear it all. The announcers, the music, the cheers of the crowd. "This is amazing."

Aiden eased up behind me, wrapping his arms around my

waist pulling me close as he pressed a kiss to my bare shoulder. He laughed when I spied a pair of binoculars, picked them up and pressed them against my eyes. A man was on first and another on third. I smiled at him over my shoulder.

"So, you like my place?" He asked, his voice low and teasing against my skin. "Worth putting up with me to see the view?"

"I'll keep fucking you until the season is over for this view," I joked, squirming away when he tickled my sides. I lowered the binoculars, turning to face him. "If you give me a hot dog, I'll stay the night."

I stilled, watching him closely to see if I'd taken it too far by inviting myself to stay, He made me comfortable and I forgot that this was weird, not my usual situation and I didn't know what he really wanted from all of this besides sex. Starting out as a murder suspect was unusual and I didn't know where to go from here. It was a couple of seconds before he moved, chuckling softly as he pressed a kiss to my temple.

"Well, lucky me." He released me and moved towards a grill nestled against the opposite wall. Aiden lifted the lid and displayed several hot dogs, their grilled perfection resting on the metal slats. "I promised you food, a game and a beer."

He dropped the lid and leaned over, pulling an ice-slick bottle from a cooler at his feet. His face was smug, triumphant and I had to laugh out loud. I took the beer he offered and took a sip of the cool liquid before peeking over his shoulder to give a significant look at the hot dogs.

"Feed me, please," I said, turning back to look at the game. I decided to clear up my confusion. Why function in the dark when I could shed some light on this situation. "So, I have to know. I this a date where we actually talk to each other or is the food and the game just a pretense for fucking?"

I watched him out of the corner of my eye. He had his

back to me, working on the grill but he paused for the briefest moment before answering.

"You're pretty direct, Doc."

I turned back to the view, needing to get all of this straight before we moved on to the rest of the evening. "You know my life, Detective and I know you don't approve. Just trying to see where I stand."

Aiden turned to face, his expression serious. Too serious for a summer night full of sultry promise.

"I don't get you but it doesn't mean that I don't want you. And I like you," he said, a smile teasing his lips. "And I think you're the one who said that you like to like the people you fuck." He shrugged. "So do I."

Okay, so that was a green light to commence the usual date get-to-know-you chat.

"How long have you lived here?" I asked.

"Since my divorce. A year ago." Aiden came up beside me, a hot dog on a paper plate with chips. It was smothered in ketchup, mustard and relish. My mouth watered and I took the plate from him. "I figured you'd like it fully loaded."

"I do," I said, taking a bite and looking back at the game for a few moments, waiting for him to return to my side to ask him more questions. "Why did you get divorced?"

"She left me for someone else. It wasn't my idea but I accepted it and moved on." His voice was even but I could sense the residual of hurt in his words. I took another bite, waiting him out to see if he would continue. He took a sip of his beer and let out a long sigh. "My job has long hours. Erratic hours. She was alone a lot."

"So, you don't blame her?"

He huffed out a sound, it wasn't a laugh but I couldn't place exactly what it was. "I blame her for not being honest with me. I blame her for cheating on me. I do understand what led her to do it."

"Understanding is the first step to forgiveness," I ventured, trying to feel out where he was in all of this. It was partly the psychiatrist but it was also the woman. I didn't want to keep walking into a situation where I was fighting the ghost of woman he still loved.

He gave me an odd look, one I had no hope of deciphering. "I don't think forgiveness is in the cards. Cheating, dishonesty." He shook his head before looking back at the game. "That's too far for me to forgive or tolerate."

I didn't know what to say. I could rattle out all my therapy guidance about forgiveness being the only way to move on but I wasn't thinking about him as a patient. This was personal.

"I don't share very well," he said, lifting the beer to his mouth and taking a long swallow.

"That could make 'us' really hard."

"Yeah. I realize that."

The silence between us wasn't awkward but it wasn't comfortable either. I struggled to find some way to move it on. When he shifted behind me and slipped his arm around my waist, I let the heat simmer between us and melt away the tension.

He rubbed his fingers across my stomach, tiny circles that widened and then contracted smaller with every few cycles. It was enticing and delicious but it wasn't satisfying. I squirmed against him, leaning over to expose my neck to his kisses as we watched the game unfolding below us on the field.

"So, how did you become a baseball fan?" He asked, leaning around to look at me. "Or are you just a Nats fan?"

I shook my head, smiling at the memories his question brought to mind. "My dad is the world's biggest baseball fan. The Mets or the Yankees, whatever game he could get tickets to, we went."

"Is he still alive?"

"My dad? Oh yeah, my folks live in Florida now. The American dream, right?" I traced my fingernail along his palm, following his lifeline along the most sensitive part. He twitched and closed his fingers over mine, raising my hand to his lips. His tender kiss on each fingertip was distracting but I kept going. "Where else could an immigrant cab driver and a school teacher send their daughter to an Ivy-League school and move to Naples when they retire?"

"Yeah? They must be proud of you."

"What about your parents? Are you from around here?"

He nodded and then we both watched the field as the home team scored a run and the crowd screamed their heads off. I jumped around, shimmying my hips in a victory dance while Aiden laughed and played it cool, taking a long swallow from his beer bottle. When I moved closer, he dragged me to him, this time chest-to-chest as he leaned against the half-wall overlooking the park. I looped my arms around his neck, pressing a soft kiss to his mouth. He tasted of beer and summer and I allowed myself a temporary deepening of the connection with a swipe of my tongue inside before pulling away to look up at him.

"So, local boy or transplant?"

"Local. I grew up in Vienna. My dad still works for the county. My mom sells real estate and spoils my sister's kids."

"Uncle Aiden?"

"Yeah, Uncle Aiden. I take them out for tattoos and picking up women."

"You do not."

"I'll never tell." He stared down at me, his large hands gripping my hips, pulling me up against the hardening bulge in his jeans. I sucked in a breath, leaning into the spike of arousal that shot up my spine and arched my back into Aiden's searching hands.

I moved in closer, running my hands over his chest, gathering his t-shirt by the hem and tugging it up. He let go of me, lifting his arms and allowing me to remove his shirt. I tossed it to the side and kissed along his collarbone, across his chest.

"You know, Bryce Harper is my favorite Nats player," I said moving away from him, playfully dodging his grasp as he reached for me. I reached up, sliding one thin strap of my sundress off my shoulder and then the other. "Did you know they have underwear with his number on it?"

He swallowed, watching my progress as I slid the other sundress strap down and off my body.

"They do?"

"They really do," I said, easing the top of my dress down, exposing my breasts to his gaze and to the air of the night. My nipples hardened and I ran a fingertip over one and then the other, arching into the pleasure radiating from the lazy tug and pinch. Aiden eased off the wall, taking a step towards me but I shook my head and he stopped with a groan of frustration that made me smile. "I bought a pair and I wear them whenever I attend a game. I bought them for luck."

I hooked the top edge of the dress and pulled it all the way down, letting the it pool on the deck underneath my feet. I stepped out of the circle of fabric, kicking off my flip-flops at the same time. Aiden's eyes roamed all over my body, his gaze hungry. One of his hands drifted down his torso and rubbed his length through his jeans, tugging and pulling on his hard, long cock.

"Maybe I should be more clear," I said running my own hand down my belly and into the panties printed on the front with the number thirty-four. I eased my fingers into my slit, unsurprised to find that I was wet. "When I wear these, it means that someone is going to get lucky."

"Fuck, you're such a little tease," Aiden growled as he advanced on me. I backed up, slowly and deliberately until I could ease myself down on a large futon couch, positioned in front of the large bank of windows of his apartment. I looked up at him, rubbing my clit underneath the fabric of my underwear, doing nothing to hide it. He watched my movements, licking his lips as his eyes roamed, his stare hungry.

"A tease doesn't let you have what's on offer. You can have it if you want it."

That's all it took and he was on top of me, his tongue in my mouth, harsh and brutal. I opened to him, crying out when his fingers joined my own underneath my panties. He pushed inside me, pumping slowly in time with the thrust of his tongue in my mouth. I bucked and the panties ripped and I cried out again, gasping into his kiss when he tugged the shards of fabric off my body.

Aiden pulled back, his expression dark and stormy, ravenous. "We can go inside if you want."

He glanced over his shoulder and at the surrounding building, windows everywhere and all of them potentially filled with voyeuristic neighbors. A thrill ran through me in a shiver and I shook my head.

"No. Let them watch. I don't care."

"Fuck yeah," he said, diving back down for my mouth but detouring at the last minute for my neck and then further down. His kisses were wet, the trail raising goosebumps on my flesh, my nipples also hard under the touch of his fingers. A pinch, a tug and I was wetter with each pulse of electricity from my breast to my clit.

Aiden slid lower, shoving my legs open, exposing me to his gaze. He ran a finger down my slit, placing it in his mouth for a long sucking, pull before burying his face between my legs and licking up and down my wet, swollen flesh.

I arched up when his teeth grazed my clit but he pushed me back down with a firm palm against my chest. He teased my nipple, squeezed my breast while he sucked and nibbled and devoured my sex. I cried out, my orgasm so close I could taste its metallic glint on my tongue.

"Such a sweet pussy. I could eat you all day and night." Another long swipe of his tongue along the length of my slit and then he left me wanting and begging again when he pulled away. "Can't get the taste of you coming off my mind. Give it to me again, baby. Please."

His ragged begging did me in and when he took my clit in his mouth again I obeyed. Long and wrenching, it was blinding bright behind my eyes and made me cry out until my voice was raw with it. My muscles aching from the tension of it. My cheeks wet from the release of it.

And then there was Aiden. Broad and heavy, draped as a solid blanket across my body as he took my mouth again, stealing my breath and making my head reel with the pleasure of it.

"Sweet. Sweet." He murmured against my skin as he rained kisses along my jaw and my cheeks. "You sweet, dirty girl. Let me fuck you."

"Yes."

What other answer was there? I'd worn my lucky panties.

Chapter Twelve

AIDEN

Carla was the sweetest temptation.

My hands shook as I kneeled between her legs, unfastening my jeans and shucking them off my body. She was long and finely boned, her skin golden and muscles tone. Her breasts were full, more than a mouth or handful and the bush between her legs was trimmed but dark. She was stretched out before me on the cushion, never attempting to cover any part of herself.

Confident in her body and her sexuality, she stole my breath and pre-occupied my mind.

"I've thought about you constantly since the other night." I leaned over her, kissing and tasting my way along her body. The spice of her inner thigh, the sweet of her nipple, the honey of her mouth. "I need to be inside you. Deep. Hard."

"Yes. I want that," she agreed, sitting up and trading spaces, pressing me back into the cushion, her body curving into my own. She scraped her nails across my chest and down my abs and I shivered under the attention and then I bowed upward when her fingers wrapped around my dick and stroked from base to tip. "Condom?"

"My jeans. In the back pocket." I let my hands roam over her body when she grabbed my jeans and pulled out the foil packet. I hit a ticklish spot and she yelped and I had to grab her and sweep over it again, loving the feel of her sweet curves undulating against me as she tried to squirm away. When she tried to bolt off the cushion, I drew her close, pressing kisses along her neck and down her spine, soothing her with touch and nonsense. "Stay. I'll be good."

"If I stay I don't want you to be good," she whispered, whimpering when I squeezed her breast, rolling her nipple in between my fingers. "Come on, Aiden. Fuck me."

"Where the hell did you come from?" I groaned out, taking the condom from her hand, opening it and rolling it down my cock. I watched as she straddled me, positioning herself over my body and lowering down until my dick was wedged deep inside her. She was hot and tight and I rocked up into her, lifting and dragging her up with my grip on her hips. "Goddam Carla, you're so fucking good."

She looked down on me, her lips curved in a wicked, knowing smile as she raised and lowered herself on my length. The buildings around us were her backdrop, the lights from the stadium her spotlight and I found myself hoping that someone was watching.

"Fuck that makes me hot," I gritted out, lifting my hips to shove my dick inside her. "I hope someone is watching. I want them to see you. So fucking gorgeous and all mine."

The possessiveness of my words made her eyes widen and I tugged her down for a kiss. Short but deep, it let her know where I stood in all this.

"You're mine for now," I whispered against her lips, emphasizing my point with several deep thrusts. "This pussy is mine. This clit is mine." I squeezed her breast, rubbing my thumb over the nipple. "This tit is mine." I lifted my hand and caressed her lips, inserting a finger for her to suck. "This mouth is mine to fill however I want." I slid my fingers around her ass cheek, finding her anus and stroking over opening, sliding my pinky inside. "This ass is mine."

"God. Yes."

"Would you let me fuck your ass Carla? Fill your hole with my cock?"

She moaned, her eyes rolling back in her head, nails digging into my chest as she rode me. Each sucking, grabbing pull of her sex on my cock brought me closer to orgasm. I wrapped my hand around her neck, holding her in place to watch me as I gave in and came.

"Carla." Heat. Fire. Fireworks. Every pulse of my dick raced through me and I flexed up into her body, milking every last aftershock for each ripple of pleasure. It was heaven and hell. I didn't care as long as I got to do it again.

She collapsed on top of me and I held her close, enjoying the feel of her heartbeat settling into its usual rhythm. When the condom needed to go, I shifted her to the side and took care of business, pulling her against me as I settled back on the cushions. The game played on below us and my neighbors did whatever they usually did on a summer evening while we settled into a comfortable silence.

"I'd like you to stay the night," I said, stating the first thing on my mind. "I hope that doesn't violate whatever rules we've got going here."

"Are there rules?' She asked, lifting herself up to lean on one elbow, smiling down at me. Her fingers brushed across my chest, hovering between ticklish and sleep-inducing. I didn't complain, I just wanted her hands on me and that was the truth. "Please explain them to me because I have no idea what I'm doing here."

"We're just seeing where this goes. Fucking, hanging out until we feel the need for a change," I said, shrugging with my own cluelessness. "I've got no idea how this works, Doc. How did it work before?"

She sighed, averting her eyes to watch the game for a while. I settled back against the cushions and waited. Nothing about this was going to be easily answered with snappy comebacks and jokes.

"It's been a long time since I had someone in my life that wasn't associated with Club D. I have partners outside of the club who I can call for a hook-up but they don't feed me and they definitely don't invite me to stay."

"You know you're pretty much every guy's fantasy, right?" When she turned back to look at me her expression was amused but also confused. I counted off the reasons on my fingers. "You like sports. You've got balls big enough to lie to the police" I gave her a glare at that one but continued. "You love sex. You belong to sex club and you're into men and women. I don't know why you don't have men banging down your door."

She laughed, throwing herself back on to the cushions beside me and landing with a huge sigh of frustration. When she slid her look back to mine, I could see a cloud of something melancholy in her expression.

"Yeah. Finding somebody to fuck me is never the problem." She shifted over onto her side, draping a long leg over mine. I wrapped my arms around her, pulling her close. This isn't where I'd thought this would go, but I was taking this ride until it ended. "Don't get me wrong. I do love sex and I love men and women and I'm healthy and I don't see any problem with doing what I want with my body."

"But?"

"But I do get tired of being seen only as a living porn video. All of those people don't see me. They see my kink and they see my sex positive lifestyle and they decide that I'm their shot at having a great story to tell the guys later when they are having beers in their man cave in suburbia."

I considered what she'd said, remembering how the men had acted during her interrogation. Juvenile. Judgmental. I hadn't been much better in the judgment department. I couldn't go back and change how that had gone down but I could make sure she had honesty from me. And respect.

Because she did.

"Well, I don't pretend to get you one-hundred percent but I fully admit that it's mostly because of my hang-ups and not you. But I think you're a badass and honest and probably the first person I've ever met who knows who they are." I leaned forward and placed a kiss on her nose, pulling back to give her as much honesty as I could in this moment. "And I don't know what the rules are or where this is going but I like you being here and I want you to stay tonight. We'll figure the rest out as we go."

Carla considered me for a moment, clearly rolling my comments around in her head and classifying me as either friend or foe.

"I'll stay," she answered, snuggling into my side and laying her head on my chest.

We settled in to watch the game for a while, living in the moment and not thinking too hard about our odds.

———

Waking up with Carla in my arms was amazing.

Drifting off last night I'd planned a lazy morning buried between her thighs with my face and my cock and making her come over and over. Feeding her and then dragging her back to bed for another round until the world intruded.

Waking up to someone banging on my door was not what I'd planned. Not one fucking bit. I slid out from under the quilt I had thrown over us last night, observing how the morning sunshine lit her skin up like gold. Her hair was a mess, testament to how much I liked to run my fingers through it and fist it as I fucked her, it took everything in me not to ignore the intruder and slide back under the covers and feast on her pussy until she moaned beneath me.

A renewed round of hammering told me that whoever it was, was not going away. I found my jeans on the deck, slid them on and padded across the deck floor, through the double doors and into my apartment. I glanced at the clock: nine in the morning.

I slid the locks open and turned the doorknob, shoving my body in the gap to prevent the person from entering. Shock at seeing just who was at my door had me stumbling back, leaving an opening that my ex-wife used to her advantage.

"Patrice, what the hell are you doing here?"

"You never answer my calls, Aiden. I had no choice," she said, tossing her purse on the counter behind me.

I reached over and picked it up, shoving it back at her. "You're not staying." I looked back over my shoulder towards my patio. Nothing about this situation was good. "I'm not alone."

"He really isn't alone but he will be if you give me five seconds."

We both spun to find Carla standing in the doorway, naked as the day she was born and completely unconcerned about anyone getting a good look. She gave a little stretch and then turned to pick her dress up off the floor before padding off towards my bathroom. I moved to follow her but the door closed with a decisive click before I got halfway across the room. I turned to face-off with Patrice.

"What the hell are you doing here?"

"I need to talk to you, Aiden," she said, her glance drifting towards the closed bathroom door.

"When she comes out of there, you're gone so spit it out," I demanded, shoving her purse towards her for emphasis. "You've got a minute or two, tops."

"I think we made a mistake."

I stopped dead, the air in the room whooshing in my ears as I tried to process the shit she'd just thrown down in my living room.

"You're out of your fucking mind. You left me for the motherfucking personal trainer at your gym, Patrice. You moved him into our house."

"I know," she said, moving towards me, her hands on my body to pull me closer. I grabbed her by the arms, pushing her away as firmly and as gently as I could. "I made a mistake, Aiden. I want to try again."

"You're crazy Patrice."

"You didn't want the divorce. You said you loved me. We could try again. Don't you want me back?"

The door to the bathroom opened and Carla stepped into the room. Her hair was pulled up into a loose ponytail, the sundress back in place along with her flip-flops. The tight smile on her face, told me that she'd heard most, if not all, of the conversation. It also told me that I was fucked.

She hurried over to where she placed her purse last night and scooped it up, nodding at Patrice as she walked between us. Carla couldn't spare me a glance but I couldn't let her go like that. I reached out for her arm but she was good at dodging me in the small space.

"Carla. Wait. She's leaving," I said, not hiding the pleading in my voice. I turned to Patrice, pointing at the door. "You're leaving."

"No, seriously. I've got to go to the Center." Carla paused at the door and threw a wave over her shoulder at me. She kept her head down but I'd had to have been blind to miss the flicker of hurt and confusion on her face. I'd promised nothing but honesty to her and this situation made me look like I wasn't living up to my end of the bargain. I wished she'd stay and let me explain but that wasn't going to happen. She wanted out and I didn't blame her. "Thanks for everything. See you around."

I watched her walk down the hallway, not taking my eyes off her until she entered the elevator. She didn't spare me another glance. I spun to face my ex-wife, irritated beyond being polite or a gentleman.

"Patrice, I don't know what you hit your head on but I'm not getting back with you. You did us in when you fucked what's-his-name in my car. What part of that do you not understand?"

She looked shocked and then hurt and then I watched in horror as a single tear rolled down her face. For a brief moment, I considered going to her and hugging her tight. I wasn't a dick but I also wasn't crazy. I'd been betrayed by this woman and she could catch herself on fire and I'd think twice about getting too close. She was poison, bad for me in every way.

I grabbed the door and opened it wide, gesturing for her to leave as she came.

"Listen, I don't know what's going on with you but I think you need to call your mom or your sister. I've got nothing here for you."

She wiped her eyes, a flare of anger making her movements jagged. She glared at me her, blue eyes flashing with hurt and embarrassment. "You don't have to be such a bastard, Aiden. This wasn't all my fault."

That struck a nerve with me and she knew it. I deflated a little, remembering all the times I'd put my job first and left her alone in our marriage. It pushed me to soften my response.

"Patrice, this isn't going to happen. I'm sorry. Stop calling me and don't come by."

"Is this because of that woman? Are you with her now? Do you love her or something?"

I started to answer that I didn't even know her but it didn't feel like the whole truth. I didn't know Carla at all really. I'd fucked her and suspected her of murder but we were still in that place where you're trying to see if there's anything there worth fighting for.

I didn't know. She was sexy and daring ad kinky as fuck. She openly spent time in other people's beds and the jealousy that accompanied the knowledge made me uncomfortable. I didn't like to share and her lifestyle was based on it. It wasn't for me but could I be satisfied with the part of her that didn't belong to Club D?

I had no fucking clue but I wasn't ready to walk away.

"She's in my life enough to ensure that there isn't room for you." I rubbed my hand over my face, wishing I could find a gentler way to tell the truth. "I'm sorry, Patrice."

She stared at me, examining me for any sign of weakness. She was still beautiful, dark hair and big blue eyes but when I looked at her I saw my past and I didn't want to go back.

"Fine, Aiden." She moved to walk out, shifting at the last minute to cup my face and kiss. There was tongue and teeth and her nails scraping sensuously across my stubble and then it was over. "You know my number if you change your mind."

Chapter Thirteen

CARLA

"Making nice with my kids will get you nowhere."

Aiden turned to face me, standing on the edge of the Anacostia Youth Center basketball court. He was sweaty, winded from playing a vigorous game with teenagers and looking sexy as hell. His strong jaw was covered in stubble but I could see a love bite I'd left on his neck and my face heated, a blush creeping over my skin. I wasn't embarrassed by what we'd done but the evidence of it here in this place was disconcerting. Usually my two worlds didn't collide and it threw me a little bit.

"I called you and texted and you didn't answer me, so I decided to come stalk you at the one place I knew you'd be at today." His grin was cocky, confident and it made me irritable. Fuck him and his sexy smile and his gorgeous ex-wife. Fuck them all.

We'd had an amazing night together, three rounds of vigorous sex and enough orgasms to make me limp with satisfaction. Aiden was a great lover and he knew his way around my body. Sexual compatibility wasn't going to be our problem.

I'd thought it would be my lifestyle but it turned out to be petite brunette with flashing blue eyes.

And my own conflicted feelings. I'd thought Aiden might be the guy who could accept all of me. He didn't get me, by his own admission, but he was trying and that was completely new and different. I'd gotten my hopes up and now I was more mad at myself than at him.

"I have no interest in getting in between you and your ex-wife, Detective," I tried to inject steel into my tone but even I heard the jealousy there. "It looks like you have some unfinished business."

I spun on my heel and headed across the empty adjacent court, planning to head back to my cubby and organize the rowing schedule for the next two weeks. Aiden caught up with me, his hand slipping around my bicep and stopping me short. I let my anger flare and jerked my arm away, drawing the attention of several of the nearby kids.

I schooled my features into and expression of calm and friendliness, , taking a deep breath. "I don't suppose that my asking you to drop it and go away would work?"

"Nope," he answered, shaking his head slowly. "The only unfinished business I have on my agenda right now, Doc, is between you and me."

His voice was low, so I was the only one who heard the sexy growl that rumbled deep in his chest. His fingertip grazed my arm and I bit back a shiver of pleasure but I couldn't stop the tell-tale fluttering of my eyelids in response to his touch. He raised an eyebrow, silently daring me to deny what was simmering between us.

I wasn't a liar and I wasn't a coward. We could hash this out like adults.

"Fine. We can talk inside."

A few minutes found us is in the short administrative hallway and I poked my head into the now vacant employee break room. It didn't have a door but in this place, this was as private as we were going to get. The center purposefully didn't have lots of doors, closed off rooms or shadowy corners where kids could get up to no good.

I hopped up on the table, watching as he strode towards me, throwing a hand out to stop him from getting too close.

"Kids everywhere. They don't need a first-hand lesson in sex education," I warned, letting my hand drop when he nodded in understanding. Aiden wasted no time in getting to the point.

"I'm not getting back together with my ex-wife and I don't know why she came to my place."

I snorted out a laugh. I knew. "She wanted to fuck you and get you back, Aiden. I got that message loud and clear from my spot in the bathroom."

"Fine. That's what she wants," he stepped forward, placing his hands on my thighs. I should have pushed him away but I didn't trust myself to actually touch him. At least this way my jeans served as a very poor barrier between me and his seductive heat. "It's not what I want."

"Don't tell me that I'm what you want? You've known me for what? A week?" I injected every word with as much derision as I could muster. I needed all of the barriers I could get between me and this man. I'd let him in just a little bit and he scared me.

"I do want you, I think you know that," he said, his tone even and calm. He wasn't rising to my bait. I wouldn't push him into a fight. He was determined to hash this out like adults. Damn it. "Forever? Hell, I don't know. For the next date? Yeah. I want that."

I shoved his hands off my body and lowered my feet to the ground. I moved by him, needing to walk.

"Aiden, I fuck other people. You've said time and time again that you don't share. We don't make sense."

He huffed out frustration, running his fingers through his sweaty hair before landing them on his hips. He focused his gaze on me and I felt like I was back in the interrogation room. I shifted on my feet and waited for whatever was coming.

"You're right. I don't get what you do."

"Yeah, you don't."

"So, explain it to me." He moved towards me, reaching out and snagging the belt loop on my jeans to pull me closer and hold me in place. The stubborn set of his jaw told me that he wasn't letting me go until I offered up something to help him understand. "You say you want a relationship someday but you sleep with all these other people. I admit it, I don't fucking get it. Did you get hurt? Are you one of the people who think monogamy is impossible?"

I eyeballed him, gauging just how much he really wanted to know. Most people talked a good game of being open-minded and free but did a lot of judging you when you told them how you lived your life. I took a deep breath and dove in. Aiden would either be here when I was done or he wouldn't.

"I'm not broken and I'm not damaged. I wasn't hurt by anyone. My parents have been happily married for almost forty years. I've loved two men and one woman in my life and I got over having my heart broken with ice cream, girlfriends and time." His lips twitched in a smile and it encouraged me to keep going. "I was in an open relationship with someone and it worked for us for a while. Sharing wasn't the problem, we just didn't love each other. We broke up and I still hung out with some of our old friends. Couples in the lifestyle who invited me to join them from time to time. I saw how it made them stronger, it fed something they needed individually and as a couple and it did the same for me. I could be in the moment with them and then walk away.

It worked. It still makes feel good so I keep doing it. I need it."

"You need it? But you come when its just the two of us. Unless you're a really great actress, you get off on it. You love it."

"I do. You make me hot and wet and insane. I love sleeping with you, Aiden and I leave completely satisfied." I struggled to really explain this part. It was hard for me to really understand. "But I need the satisfaction I get when I'm with other couples. I don't know why but I know that it latches onto something in my gut and brings me contentment. It's visceral, in my bones. I can't explain it except that for now its part of who I am. I want you to understand but I'm not going to apologize or be ashamed of something I need for myself."

He shifted from foot to foot and I watched him process what I'd just said. I didn't have much more to add so I'd wait for him to ask the questions that bugged him the most.

"So, these couples, how do they know how to find you?"

"At first it was private groups on the internet but for the past four years, I've been a member of Club D. My couples are all members and they keep me busy and fulfilled." I shrugged my shoulders not sure what else I could add. "It's my kink. I'd like to have a relationship with one person one day, a man or woman of my own but they'd have to accept all of me."

I didn't have to tell him just how much I longed for that. My voice gave me away, the hitch that I tried to hide but failed. I was happy. I was content with my life. But I was alone and it wasn't by choice.

"And that includes your kink," he said, his gaze level and expression blank. I couldn't read his mind. I could only tell him what was on mine.

"Yes. That includes my kink." I let a couple of moments

passed before I asked the question on my mind. "So, are you in or out?"

He tugged on my belt loop, moving me the three steps necessary to close the distance between us. He opened his mouth to say something, closed it and then shook his head with a laugh.

"I think I'm crazy."

"I don't know what that means," I needed him to say it out loud.

"It means I'm in," he said, leaning down to press a soft kiss to my mouth. "I feel like I've lost my mind but I'm in. I just can't walk away right now."

His words made my stomach clench and not in the best way but I understood. And I appreciated his honesty, more than I could say. I rolled an idea around in my mind, debating whether to offer. He was a big boy. He'd had no trouble telling me exactly where he stood on every other issue, I trusted that he'd do the same now.

"Why don't you come to the Club with me?"

"Huh, What?"

"On some nights you can bring a guest. They'll do a simple background check on you but that shouldn't be a problem. It's usually slower because some people only want to play with members."

He took a step back, not a big one but enough to make his hesitance evident. "I don't think I'm into playing with other people, Carla. That's not my thing."

"No. I didn't mean that we would go to do that." I closed the distance between us again, laying my hand on chest. His heart was pounding. I just didn't know if it was because he was turned on or scared. "We could play together. You like to be watched, yeah?" When he nodded, I continued. "We could go, see if you're feeling it and if you are . . ."

"People could watch?" His voice was breathy and he swallowed hard. His heart rate picked up and I knew it wasn't from fear this time. He was getting hard and I could feel it, pressed against my belly where my own muscles clenched in anticipation.

"It would be hot." I leaned up to press a soft kiss against his lips, making sure my eyes told him that this was completely up to him. "The two of us. Under the stars again. Exploring our kinks together."

He grinned and my breath caught at the feral twist to his lips. "I'm in."

Chapter Fourteen

AIDEN

Club D was in an old mansion just outside of DC, hidden behind ornate gates and lots of security.

It had been a couple of weeks since Carla had invited me and I'd agreed. Exploring our kinks together was sexy as fuck but it also seemed like a good way to get to know the woman who had been spending a lot of time in my bed.

When she wasn't in someone else's bed.

After several weeks of navigating seeing each other around work and her couples, she'd invited me again and I'd agreed.

It was important to her and so it was becoming important to me. It wasn't easy knowing she was off with other people those nights but I was trying to curb my jealousy. Seeing it with my own eyes had to be better than what I concocted in my mind.

"It looks like a resort," I murmured in her ear as we exited the mansion and entered a pool area that rivaled the most expensive vacation spots.

Lounge chairs circled all sides of the large, lighted pool, each one sitting next to a side-table with a sun umbrella nearby. The cushions were coordinated in the Club D colors of navy blue and white and were embroidered with the logo.

Several bars circled the area and a huge, a covered eating area was to the right and just behind the house. To the left of the pool was all kinds of lush greenery and flowers, the evening lights shining up from hidden spaces also cast a glow in the massive hot tub where several nude couples currently laughed and sipped on drinks. They glanced in our direction, some of them waving to Carla who returned the greeting.

She smiled, her arm laced with my own as she led me over to the bar. "This is a place where we can all come to relax and completely be ourselves. It's a vacation from our everyday lives so it should feel that way." She pointed all around the space as I took our drinks. "Over there are the private outdoor beds and the play area."

"They are open for use by anyone?"

"Yes. Anyone and anytime."

"Carla, I have something for you." We both turned to look at a beautiful woman who approached us with a smile to go with her British accent. Her blonde hair gleamed under the evening lights but her smile was warm. The large, dark man at her side wasn't smiling, his demeanor aloof but not unfriendly.

I thought I knew who they were, the best friend and the mercenary husband. Members of the lifestyle. They'd been off to Paris and I hadn't had a chance to meet them. It looked like tonight was the night.

"Livvy! Rush!" Carla let go of me to hug the woman and accept a kiss on the cheek from the man. She turned and took my hand in her own, making the introductions. "This is Aiden."

"It's so great to meet you, Aiden," Livvy leaned forward, pressing a kiss to my cheek. Her white dress was see-through, her nipples and pubic area dark underneath the flimsy fabric.

I let my gaze linger, a move noted by her husband. I expected to get a fist in my face but he merely smirked, slipping his huge paw of hand around her waist. "I have your bracelets."

"Bracelets?" I asked, confused even more when handed over two made of braided green silk. Carla took my wrist, tying one of them on me before handing the second one to me and holding out her own wrist.

"The green tells everyone that we're not sharing. They'll know that we're here only to play with each other." She slid me look that held heat and a hint of a tease. "If you change your mind, all you have to do is take it off."

I held her gaze, knowing that she was just explaining the rules. We'd talked about tonight and she'd let me set the boundaries. I liked being watched and it was a fantasy of mine but I wasn't on board to join into group sex. Carla had assured me that it was likely to happen as the night progressed but that no one would overstep our rules.

The bracelet was the signal. I glanced at Rush's wrists. He wore a metal chain, a red disc suspended from one of the links. He saw where I was looking and answered the question before I could ask it.

"The red disc says that we're open to play." He held out the bracelet for my inspection. "We actively live the lifestyle so we had our own bracelets made."

"And you're okay with it? Sharing. Watching other people fuck your wife?" I asked the question, wondering too late if I'd gone too far.

"Yeah. It gets me off. And I know she might share her body with other people but I've got her heart and soul and that's all that matters in the end." He shrugged. "Different strokes man. Variety is the fucking spice of life."

I turned to find Carla and stopped dead in my tracks. She was dancing with Livvy, her dark hair and golden skin in stark but gorgeous contrast to the pale tones of her friend. In a black dress that dipped down to her navel and barely covered her ass cheeks, Carla's long legs in her sky-high fuck-me heels looked like they went on for miles. They were laughing, just like two women would do in any club. Enjoying the music and the night out with their friend.

"I fucking love spice," I told Rush, taking a sip from my drink as I watched them move together. He grunted in agreement next me, his large body settling onto a barstool to watch the show.

And it was definitely a performance and clearly for our benefit. The women, our women, ran their hands all over each other, moving as one to the sensual music piping out from the hidden speakers. Their heads dipped towards each other, lips brushing, a flash of tongue before they kissed in earnest. It didn't last long but Livvy's cheeks were flushed when they parted and she laughed. Carla glanced at me over her shoulder, her gaze questioning and I nodded, letting her know that it was okay.

It more than okay. It was fucking hot. I reached down and adjusted my cock under my dark dress pants. I was hard, aching. The usual state of my dick when Carla was around.

"You doing okay, man?" Rush's voice interrupted my focus and I looked over at him. His eye was on his wife but he kept talking. "I know you're not into the lifestyle."

"I'm figuring it out," I answered, taking another long sip of whiskey from my glass before answering. "For her. I'm figuring shit out for Carla."

"She's worth it." Rush said, squeezing my shoulder as he passed by, slipping up behind his wife and tipping her head back for a long, slow kiss. He reached out blindly and Carla put her hand in his, smiling up at him when he kissed her fingers and bowed before pulling his wife away towards the hot tub.

He wasn't telling me anything I didn't already suspect was

true. Carla was one-in-a-million. I just didn't know if I could pay the price.

I came up behind Carla, grabbing her hips and spinning her around to face me. She leaned up and kissed me, wrapping her arms around my neck as our tongues tangled for dominance. She giggled and I smiled down at her, enjoying the feel of her in my arms and her focus solely on me. I was possessive of her, not something I had to hide. Carla wanted it all. She wanted to know everything I was feeling good or bad. We both knew it was the only way to do what we were doing.

We swayed to the music, her body brushing against my cock with every movement and I was getting harder by the second. I groaned, breaking off the kiss to catch my breath and press kisses all along the soft column of her neck.

Movement behind us caught my eye and I lifted my head, soaking in the erotic scene playing out in front of us. Livvy and Rush had discarded their clothes and were in the hot tub, Rush kissing her breasts as a woman took her mouth. Their hands were interwined, tender in the way that it maintained their connection even while others joined them for a time.

"Aren't they beautiful?" Carla asked, her lips tracing a path down my chest as she unbuttoned my shirt.

"Are they one of yours?"

She looked up at me, her eyes a little wary at my question. I'd suspected the answer but never asked. "Yes. They are."

I looked down at her, waiting for the jealousy to rip through me. There was a twinge but not enough for me to stop touching her, to walk away from her. But I wasn't going to deny my need to make my own mark on her life, her soul.

"I want to fuck you, Carla." I slid my hand under hair, circling the back of her neck to hold her in place. I tugged the strands a little harder, loving the gasp that escaped form between her parted lips. My reaction was visceral, primal and

I didn't even try to rein it in. She had to know what she did to me and I couldn't be afraid of showing the good, the bad and the neanderthal. "You're mine tonight and I want them to know."

"Come on," she said, taking my hand in hers and leading me across the patio to the space holding the private play areas. It wasn't what I'd expected. It was beautiful, sensual, decadent. The space was filled with canopied, four poster beds, the sides and tops draped with white, sheer strips of gauze. They moved in the slight breeze of the evening, the muted lights flickering with the sway of the trees surrounding the area.

There were several beds already occupied. Couples and foursomes, naked bodies moving together as they moaned and whispered and laughed, their sounds muted by the night. I couldn't peel my gaze away from them, the raw erotic sensuality of the scene making my dick ache and my heart pound in my chest.

I followed her deeper into the maze of beds and bodies, drinking it all in. I hadn't known I was thirsty for this but I couldn't get enough of the electric desire in the balmy air around us. We stopped in front of a bed, king-sized and covered in crisp, white linens. It overlooked the hot tub and pool, it's position would allow everyone in those places to see us. It was my fantasy. She'd delivered it to me on a platter and all I had to do was feast.

This woman was like no one I had ever met before and I winced at the thought that I might never have.

I buried my fingers in Carla's hair, holding her still as I plunged my tongue into her mouth, plundering, demanding, wet and hot as I poured my lust and need into the kiss wanting to have all of her, right now. She whimpered and my dick ached, throbbing in the confines of my pants. I gentled our connection, pressing my lips to her cheeks, her eyelids, the tip of her nose.

"Thank you, baby." I lowered my hands, slipping under the thin straps of her slip of a dress and easing them off her shoulders and down her arms. "Thank you for this."

The weight of the silken fabric pulled it down and over her body, settling in a black pool at her feet. She wasn't wearing any underwear, just the heels and I wanted them to stay on for the moment. I pressed down lightly on her shoulders and she glided down to her knees, her grace and beauty robbing my breath. She lifted her face, gazing up at me, her expression making it clear that she was waiting for my orders.

I left her there, kneeling at my feet in the puddle of her clothing and took one step backward. She frowned slightly but I shook my head and she stopped immediately. Carla wasn't always submissive but when she was, it was a gorgeous sight.

"Good girl," I said, beginning the slow process of removing my own clothes. Carefully, precisely, teasingly I removed every item. The crisp cotton dress shirt, my pants, underwear, shoes and socks ended up in a neat pile near the bed. I took my time dragging out the anticipation building between us and the crowd watching us from the hot tub.

I didn't concentrate on them, a brief glance took them all in and invited them to enjoy at the same time. Carla was beautiful, brave, confident and true to herself. I intended to show them all how she should be worshipped. My fantasy come to life with her in the starring role.

I shifted my attention back to her, closing the distance to stand right in front of her. She looked up at me from where she kneeled, her gaze drifting down to focus on my dick. I reached down, taking the length in my fist, giving it a slow deliberate stroke which brought it within licking distance of her mouth. Carla slipped her tongue out and swiped along the head, her grin wicked when I gasped at the sensation.

"Witch," I gritted out, sliding my fingers in the silk of her hair and urging her forward. "Suck me."

Carla opened wide and I slid inside, locking my knees when the wet heat of her mouth raced through me and made weak. It was so damn good. Every. Fucking. Time.

"Fuck, you're so good at that, baby," I groaned out, tipping my head back and taking in the canopy of stars above us the dark, clear sky. I lowered my lids, concentrating on the feel of her mouth on me, on the knowledge that this was Carla. The woman who'd rocked my world the minute I'd laid eyes on her.

She sucked me, her silky hair tickling my belly and raising goosebumps on my skin. I shivered, not just from the cold but also the start of my orgasm in my groin. Too soon. Way too fucking soon.

I lowered my head and reached out, caressing her soft skin as I pulled out of her mouth. She opened her eyes and gazed up at me under lids, half-closed with lust. She was drunk on us, a feeling I knew very well whenever I was with her.

"Come here," I said, leaning down to gather her close, dipping my head to take her mouth in a gentle kiss. It was long and intense, tender and deep. She moaned and I moved her backwards, breaking the contact only to drape her across the bed.

I took a step back, taking in her long, taut body stretched over the crisp, white sheets. Hair fanned out in a tousled halo around her face, nipples tight peaks in the cool of the evening, long legs ending in the gorgeous "V" of her dark bush.

"You're so fucking beautiful. Do you have any idea?" I asked, my voice rough and chest tight. She smiled, wicked and sultry, and my heart skipped a couple of beats. Not for the first time, she had me speechless. It didn't matter, she told me exactly what she wanted.

With one hand, she traced down between her breasts and across her belly, stopping only with her fingers buried in the slickness of her pussy.

"Why don't you show me how beautiful you think I am?"

———

CARLA

I would never get tired of Aiden looking at me like I was fucking edible.

And I loved it when he settled between my legs and ate at me like a starving man. Some men came at you like they were afraid you were going to break but Aiden grabbed my ass cheeks in both hands and held me down while he tasted, licked, sucked and probed every inch of my pussy.

I writhed against him, loving the prickly feel of his stubble in contrast with the wet velvet of his tongue. He sucked on my clit, fucking me slowly with two fingers, hitting all the spots inside me that made me grind and whimper with the sweet torture of it all. I ran my fingers over my skin, now damp with the heat of the evening and my sweat, lingering over the fullness of my breast and the tight nub of my nipples.

The first tingle of my orgasm had my thighs clenching around his head, my fingers tangled in his hair. I pulled, lifting his mouth off me. He let loose a feral growl and stared up at me with eyes glittering with his desire.

"I want you to fucking come on my mouth. I want it." He tried to lower his head again but I kept my grip on his hair and I was rewarded with sharp nip of his teeth on my inner thigh. I yelped, writhing when he soothed the spot with sweet, sloppy kisses that traveled upward to the sensitive crease of my hip.

Biting my lip, I begged. "I want you to fuck me. I want to come with you inside me Aiden, please."

He was a goner when I begged and I used it shamelessly to get what I wanted. And right then I wanted him inside me.

Aiden levered off me, reaching over to the basket of supplies placed in the middle of our play area and grabbed a condom, quickly rolling it on his dick. He shifted back to my side and slapped my ass, the tingles of pain and pleasure mixing to make me squirm in anticipation.

"Roll over. Hands and knees, baby." I hesitated for a split second and then did as I was told, allowing him to manhandle me into the position he wanted.

Aiden ran his fingers lightly over my ass and then upwards along my spine, winding them in my hair at the nape. The sharp tug backward surprised me and I gasped as my head came up and I found myself gazing at the group watching from the hot tub. I moaned, my thighs clenching with the raw arousal that shot through me.

"Open up baby," Aiden groaned, draping his hard body over my back. His hand insinuated itself between my thighs, spreading me open to the exploration of his touch and the cool night air. His cock pressed against my slit and I pushed back, needing him to fill me up. Aiden slid inside, hard and deep, I squirmed encouraging him to move, to do something.

"Keep looking at them, Carla." Aiden murmured against my ear, his hand cupping my jaw and holding my face in place. I had no choice but to look at our voyeurs, taking in their heated glances and sensual activity. "Watch them as I fuck you, baby. They've never seen anything like you before." He started to move inside me then, his words honey slick and arousing. "So goddam gorgeous. So dirty. So hot for it."

"Hot for you," I gasped out in between his thrusts, each one stealing my breath and driving me closer to my orgasm. "Just fucking wet and hot for you."

"Oh, you fucking kill me. So sweet. So sticky sweet. I can't enough of you," he panted against my cheek, his breath growing more ragged with each slam of his dick inside me. He nudged my face again, making sure I was watching the crowd below us. "Do you see them? Touching each other? Tasting and fucking? They can't take their eyes off you and you're going to make them come." He raised himself up, his hands gripping both my shoulders as he increased his speed and depth, driving me forward with each snap of his hips. "You're going to make me come. Jesus."

I was close too. Balancing myself of one arm, I reached down between my legs and found my clit, rubbing it in rhythm with his thrusts. I could feel him sliding in and out of me. The group before me was writhing together, kissing and fondling, sucking and fucking, many of their gazes focused on us. My own little porno while we gave them a show.

Aiden leaned over me again, biting the sweet spot on my neck and I let go. Wave after wave of pleasure washed over me and my knees gave out. I fell forward onto the bed, Aiden pounding into me as I came, his cock going deeper at this angle and drawing out my orgasm for what seemed like an impossibly long time. His fingers dug into my hips and I heard him shout my name and then go still, buried inside me. His thighs shook, breathing ragged and shallow as he groaned into my hair, holding me close.

"Thank you. Thank you, baby," Aiden murmured against my neck, his lips soft and tender against my skin. "Thank you," he whispered again against my skin. I took his hand, intertwining our fingers together because I didn't want our connection to end.

"For bringing you here?"

"Yes," he nodded, nuzzling sweetly against my neck. "For that. For sharing yourself with me. For giving me a chance."

I snuggled into his grasp, cherishing this moment with a man who could accept me and share his own fantasies with me. There was no space between us. No room for doubt. No room for difference. Only the two us exploring pleasure and boundaries together.

Chapter Fifteen

AIDEN

It had been a long ass day and I was grateful for the hot shower.

Carla was out with one of her couples and I'd stayed late at the office, wrapping up some paperwork on the Marsden case and then had headed downstairs the to the stationhouse gym for a workout. Peter had gone home to have dinner with Katie and the girls but I'd found a sparring partner in a big guy from the vice unit. It had me loose and relaxed and ready to head home and go to bed after I caught up on the game scores.

A group of guys from homicide came into the locker room, sweaty and raucous from a pick-up basketball game. I nodded at them, pulling on my t-shirt and tucking it into the waistband of my jeans, I sat on the bench to pull on my boots.

"Hey Cross," Detective Hunt shouted from across the room and I turned, hoping that he made this quick. He was good cop but a pain in the ass and I really didn't like him. This profession was full of assholes, it was a quality that made you a good cop but not good at much else.

"Yeah, Hunt? What the fuck man, I'm getting out of here."

He exchanged a look with the guy standing next to him, the meaning of it indecipherable to me. I turned back to slipping in my boots, demonstrating the number of fucks I didn't give.

"You running home to see that doctor? Is it your night to fuck her or are you going home to beat off?" I stopped my progress, turning to eyeball him from across the room and give him one last chance to re-think where this was going. "You have a calendar? You get her ass on Mondays and Wednesdays"

I launched myself at him, tackling him with a shove to the middle. He went down like a tree and I went with him. Both of us landing with a teeth-rattling thud on the concrete floor. Hunt thrashed beneath me, landing a decent punch into my side. I grunted and leveraged my larger bulk on top of him, getting a few punches of my own before his buddy wrenched me off him.

Dazed and on my back, I wasn't ready when Hunt kicked out and caught me in the gut. I doubled over, coughing and heaving as I rolled away and struggled to my feet. I steadied myself for a brief moment, facing off at him and debating on how far I was going to take this.

"She's a whore, Cross. I guess I should congratulate you on getting the pussy for free when everyone else has to pay," he taunted, wiping at the small dribble of blood on his lip.

I struck out without thinking, landing a punch on his jaw and sending his head snapping back as he staggered into the lockers behind him. While he was trying to orient himself, I went for him again, this time with both fists in whatever place I could reach. I kept waiting for the thud of my body hitting his to lessen the anger boiling in my gut but it never did.

Only the voice of the Captain stopped my violence. Hands dragged me off Hunt, who was still standing with the support of his buddy. His lip was split open and he was going to have a back-eye and I couldn't give a fuck.

"Cross. Hunt. What the hell is going on here?"

The room got very quiet as all the men around us pretended to be anywhere but here. I wiped at my nose with the back of my hand, disgusted by the blood I found there. I didn't remember the asshole getting in a punch to my face.

"Cross, you want to explain what's going on here?" The Captain asked, his voice low and threatening. He wasn't going to tolerate fighting amongst his men but he wasn't going to like my answer any better. I wasn't a rat,

I glanced at Hunt, weighing my options and going for the only that was viable. "Hunt is a fucking Yankees fan. I tried to beat the stupid out of him." I tossed another disgusted glance at my opponent. "I don't think it worked."

Hunt made a move towards me but his buddy held him back, murmuring stuff about "another time" and "letting it go".

The Captain transferred his attention to him, his glare just as fierce. "Is that true, Hunt?"

"About being a Yankees fan?" He asked, shaking off the restraints from his friends.

"No, about you being stupid." A loud snicker rose up from someone in the room but a glare from the Captain made it stop immediately.

Hunt paused, his gaze lingering over the face of the boss and wondering how to play this. Our fight could get us both some unpaid time off. The real reason why we were fighting could get us so much more than that.

Hunt took a long time to eyeball me before he nodded. "Yeah. Cross doesn't know a good team when he sees one."

The Captain gave us both a long look and then let his eyes

travel around the room. Grown men suddenly became very interested in the ceiling tiles or their shoes. When he returned his gaze to us, he scattered everyone with a bark.

"Then get your asses home or back to work." When I tried to shuffle past him he stopped me with a hand on my shoulder. "You alright Cross?"

I nodded. "It was nothing, sir. Just a misunderstanding."

"Sometimes our personal lives can impact our job. People don't always understand other folk's choices and feel the need to comment on them. When you choose a controversial path, it comes with the territory and you've got to decide to let it go or fight it at every turn. Just remember that it was your choice to begin with and if you care so much about what people think, then maybe it wasn't the right one." He cast me a meaningful glance that told me he knew exactly what the fight had been about. "Or it's just not the right one for you."

I watched him leave the locker room, his words ringing in my ears. It was clear that he'd known exactly what the fight had been about. Carla was never going to be an easy choice and the fact that everyone in my workplace knew everything about her life was going to be something I had to live with.

I didn't like people to know my business. My divorce had been bullpen fodder for months. My wife had cheated on me and left me. It didn't matter that half the department was divorced. I was the cuckold and the fool and it still got under my skin and made my blood boil.

I told myself that Carla wasn't cheating on me. I knew where she was and while I might not know who she was with, I understood the parameters. That was Club D stuff and our time together was something altogether different. But it bothered me and I couldn't deny it.

I put my boots on, cleaning up my face and clothes as best I could and left the precinct. When I got to my car I sat there for a long time, staring out the windshield but seeing nothing that made sense of the turmoil in my mind. I checked the time. It was late and I knew Carla would be home.

It wasn't my night but I needed to see her. Needed to ground myself in what we had and how well it was working.

Traffic was light and I made it to her place in less than thirty minutes, pulling into a curbside spot to make my final decision. I opened the window and peered up at her floor, noting the darkness in her windows. She wasn't home or she'd gone to bed and I had a decision to make. To stay or to go . . . That was the question.

A black Lincoln town car pulled up in front of her building and the back door opened, two people spilling out onto the sidewalk in a babble of laughter and good night chatter. A mans and a woman, they were joined by a third person, a man dressed in expensive casual clothing that screamed money even in the gloom of the evening.

The woman tossed her hair back over her shoulder and I paused, recognizing the movement and then the figure. Carla was smiling, her hand resting on the forearm of one of the men as he said something that they all thought was funny.

I didn't. I was anything but amused.

I knew I should keep my ass in the car but I also knew it wasn't going to happen.

Jealousy. Anger over the fight I'd just had. Fury at myself for rising to the goddam bait and letting some asshole like Hunt make me doubt myself and Carla. All of it propelled me out of the car on autopilot and down the sidewalk to the unsuspecting group.

One of the men looked up, tracking my approach and moved Carla out of my direct path. He was protecting her and I should have been grateful but I wasn't. I was pissed and I fed all of that into the shove I leveled at his chest that knocked him out of the way.

I reached for her but she jerked out of range, her face shocked and afraid.

It was the fear that stopped me in my tracks.

But it didn't stop my mouth.

"Who are these people, Carla?" When she didn't answer fast enough I snarled it out again, nice and slow. "Who. Are. These. People.?"

She stared at me, incomprehension marring her beautiful features. Her hair was loose around her shoulders and she wore a yellow sundress with flowers sewn along the edges of the skirt. Her heels were high as usual and she looked delicious and sweet and enticing.

I knew in my gut that she'd spent the evening with these men and it made me crazy. I gritted my teeth, my fingernails digging into my palms with the pressure from my tight fist.

"Aiden, you need to go. This is neither the time nor the place," she directed, turning on the icy tone I remembered from our first few encounters.

It reminded me of a time before I'd kissed her, before I'd slid inside her, before I'd made her come apart in my arms. It hurt and I only knew one way to make myself feel better.

I needed to hurt her.

I motioned to the two men hovering protectively around her, daring them with a glance just to give me one reason to take a punch. "Did you sleep with them?"

Her face went blank, anger sparking the deep honey of her eyes. "No, Aiden. I fucked them. There's a difference. I thought you knew that by now."

"There's a difference?" I asked stupidly, stubbornly refusing to concede one inch on whatever point I was trying to make. "Do you even know the difference?"

"Yes, and the fact that you don't is the problem."

I scoffed, the sound bitter and ugly like my mood. "The fact you think there is a difference is the problem. You just like to get fucked by lots of people. However, you want to package it means nothing in the end. It's just getting laid, sweetheart and that's all it means."

"No. It just means that we're over." She backed up and around her companions, digging for her keys in her purse as she headed towards her door. The lamplight caught her face and I saw the tears, wet and streaking her cheeks with makeup.

My heart screamed for me to follow her and take it all back. I moved forward but one the men on the sidewalk stopped me, his stern expression telling me that he would put up with no more shit from me.

"I don't who you are but we all have that one moment in our life that we're going to look back on and regret it for the rest of our lives." He pushed against my chest with one finger, the pity on his face almost unbearable. "This is it for you, buddy. This is it."

And I knew he was right.

Chapter Sixteen

CARLA

Sometimes you just know when shit is not right.

I'd been pre-occupied and an all-around bitch ever since Aiden had decided to show his asshole-true-colors. Actually, he'd thrown up warning flags from the minute I'd met him. Only my lust and desire for some sort of personal connection muddied the waters I usually have no trouble swimming in.

But I knew the minute I opened my front door that there was somebody in my house and things were about to get worse. As it had been my usual state over the past week I'd been distracted. I'd been thinking Aiden. I missed him. I missed him in my life. I missed his body in my bed. I missed his hands all over me.

He'd been pretty clear a couple of days ago the we had no future and that I'd spent the past few weeks concocting a fantasy in my head that he'd wanted to be the one that I could build a life with. I had thought that Aiden was the guy who could accept me. Everything about me. My long hours at work, my dedication to my kids and my kink. I'd been wrong. It had come down to the moment of truth where he was confronted with what it really meant to be with me he couldn't do it.

It didn't make him a bad person.

My kink didn't make me a bad person either.

It just meant that we couldn't find a place where we would work. People spent a lot of money and time on my couch to learn the lesson I'd just learned. I just needed to move on, I needed to stop thinking about it and I needed to stop thinking about what we might've had if it had been different.

All of this had been stewing in my brain when I'd opened the front door and found Davina sitting on my couch. She looked gaunt, spent. She looked like a woman who was at the end of her tether. And I meant the tether that kept her chained to any level of sanity.

As a psychiatrist, I tried not to think in terms of crazy or any other kind of slang to describe mental illness but sometimes it was the only way to sum up the depth of instability. I took one look at her face and I knew that if I looked up the phrase "bat shit crazy" in the urban dictionary, Davina's picture would be right next to it holding the gun she had pointed at my heart.

I took a step back on instinct trying to put whatever distance I could between me and the woman was clearly going to kill me but she was one step ahead of me.

"Don't move," she said. "Don't move you home-wrecking little cunt."

Her hand shook, the gun unsteady, but it remained focused always on me. I looked around me, searching for a place to escape. But there wasn't any place for me to run to, no place to hide in my front hall. Built like a bowling alley, the distance between us was a straight shot. Even if I bolted with all I had in me, there was no way to get past her and no way to get back out of the front door. My only choice was to go forward but my feet wouldn't move in that direction. It was walking straight into a loaded gun and I wasn't the crazy one.

"Davina put the gun down. Somebody's going to get hurt. We can talk about this," I said, trying to use my best shrink voice. It was calculated to keep her calm and her finger off the trigger.

It didn't work.

The shot she pulled off was brittle and terrifying as it cracked across the silence of my home. I ducked, getting as low as possible while keeping my eyes on her. Talking wasn't going to work. I was going to have to act. Whatever I was going to try it wasn't going to talk her out of whatever decision she'd made. But right now, all I had was my voice and years of training and a prayer that it would work.

"Davina put the gun down." I slowly inched forward, eliminating any sudden movement which might make her pull the trigger again. If I could get to the living room without a bullet between my eyes, I could run for a place to lock myself behind a very sturdy door. "Davina listen to me, you've already killed two people. You don't want to do it again."

She just stared at me as if she was trying to process the information and I wondered what in the world could possibly be going through her head right now.

"Davina listen to me. I'm sure my neighbors heard the shot and called the police. You already killed two people and this will only make it worse. The cops aren't going to let you shoot me. They'll have to hurt you and I don't want that. We were friends once. I don't want you to get hurt."

Her voice was calm and steady, her laugh brittle and off-killter. "We weren't friends. If I wanted to keep my husband I had to let him fuck you and you had to try and take him from me."

I shook my head, continuing my slow journey towards the living area. "I didn't. You know me, I'd never do that."

She wasn't listening to me, her rambling was a constant loop of nonsense and pain.

"He wanted you. I didn't kill you right away because you said no but I know you are part of the problem. I can't let you do this to someone else, some other woman." I groaned and swallowed down the bile that rose in my throat. She thought shooting me was part of a larger crusade and that meant I was screwed. It wasn't about me, I was just the first step. "Nathan broke his promise and some other man at the club will do the same. They just want to fuck younger, prettier women. It's just an excuse."

I held my hands up and realized just how futile how cliché it was. But I was so close the place where I could run and I just needed to keep her talking.

"Davina, I know I know he broke a promise to you and I'm so sorry. But I turned him down because you are my friend and I would never hurt you like that. Don't punish me for something I didn't do. Please."

"I don't care Carla. I don't care," she chanted, shaking her head back and forth with vehemence. "I can't have you here anymore. You can't be here. I tried to be sexy like you. I tried to be funny and smart but all he could see was you and how I wasn't you. I lived up to my end of the bargain but he wanted you."

I smashed myself against the wall as I neared the end of the hallway, sliding towards the opening. I closed my eyes, counting off in my head as I willed my legs to move and take me to a place of relative safety. I envisioned the large, heavy island, knowing that if I could get behind it then I could make a run for the bathroom.

I took a deep breath and opened my eyes.

I ran.

The shot went off behind me, spraying drywall all over the

side of my face as I bolted for the kitchen. I hit my marble floor on my knees and slid behind the block of wood and granite. I dug in my purse for my phone and dialed 9-1-1 and left it on the floor wedged under the lip of the cabinet. I couldn't trust myself not to turn off the call with my trembling fingers and this way the call would remain open for them to send help.

I peeked over the edge of the countertop as the voice of the operator rang out through the speaker on my phone. Davina stilled at the moment the noise broke the relative silence of fear and ragged breathing. I was scared and worried that I was out of options, so I went for broke and yelled.

"Davina Marsden is trying to kill me. My name is Carla Androghetti. Send help now!"

She decided to come at me then and I jumped to my feet, and circled in the opposite direction, keeping the island between us. I spotted the drawer holding the knives and yanked it open, grabbing the biggest one I could find in a glance. I ignored the cuts on my fingers as I pawed through the drawer and the thought that I was literally bringing a knife to a gunfight made me snort out a dark laugh. I gripped the weapon as tightly as I could in hands slick with sweat and held it in front of me as I faced off my enemy.

She lunged at me, firing off another shot that went wild and hit somewhere behind me and I took the opportunity to slash the blade against the skin of her forearm. Blood was everywhere and when she cried out, I struck again and again. She dropped the gun and I took off at a run, headed straight for my bathroom.

I slid on the marble floor but I kept going, throwing my body into the opening and shoving the door closed and slamming the lock home with a speed that surprised me. It was a thick door and I hoped it would hold for a little while, at least until the cops arrived. Shots hit the door and I flinched, covering my body as much as I could. The bullets buckled the wood but didn't penetrate but I couldn't count on that for long. I had no idea how many bullets she had or how long I'd be trapped in this room.

I looked around for a better place to hide, wedging myself in the narrow gap between the toilet and the sink cabinet. Davina banged on the door, screaming like the crazy woman she clearly was and firing shots at random. Every word that left her mouth was coated with frustration and desperation and I covered my ears to block her out. It was cowardly but I just couldn't listen any longer. I knew that I would never ever get that the sound of her frantic high-pitched screaming out of my head. I held the knife out in front of me as a talisman against her particular brand of evil, her blood running down my hands and making it difficult for me to keep hold of the weapon but I wasn't going to let it go.

I sunk to the floor, my knees pulled up against my chest, shaking and trying not to cry while hoping and straining to hear the sounds of the police or somebody coming to help me. I thought of Aiden and that night on his roof with the Nats playing in the background while he made me feel accepted and wanted. I thought about the future I thought we were going to have together and the way it had all blown apart.

I didn't regret my time with him, didn't regret taking a chance. Not on him.

Davina's screaming faltered and then there was a crash and more voices. Shots. More yelling. Male voices yelling at her to get down on the floor, to put the gun down. I stayed in the bathroom huddled against the cabinet unwilling to open the door just in case my frightened hysterical brain had somehow fooled me into believing that help had finally come.

And then I heard his voice.

Aiden.

Aiden calling to me through the door, banging on the wood and shaking the handle, begging for me to open the door and let him in. I wanted to move but I couldn't. So, I waited where I was because I knew he would come and get me and hold me and make all of this horror fade away. I knew he would do this because while he couldn't have a relationship with me, he would never let me get hurt or suffer alone. He was a cop down to his marrow, pledged to protect and serve. Even if he couldn't love.

"Carla! Carla! Baby can you hear me?" He banged on the door and shook the doorknob again. "Baby, it's me. It's Aiden. Open the door."

I couldn't move but I heard myself cry out. I was painful and completely involuntary. It was broken and scared and I guess he heard it too because the next thing I knew he was breaking down the door and looking down to where I was huddled with the knife clutched to my chest. He knelt down in front of me, his hands extended in a calming gesture.

"Carla, baby, give me the knife. We've got Davina and you're fine. It's okay. Just give me the knife."

I stared at him. I couldn't really comprehend what he was saying I just wanted it all to be over. I felt lightheaded, the adrenaline rushing out of my body and I held the weapon out to him, watching in a daze as it fell from my grasp and clattered to the floor. Aiden kicked it to the side and then he was pulling me close, into his lap as he settled back against the wall.

My face was pressed against his chest where I could feel the steady frantic beat of his heart, feel the warmth of his body, and smell the lingering scent of his aftershave and the detergent he used on his T-shirt. Familiar. Safe. His lips pressed against my temple, soft and gentle and kind as he murmured nonsense over and over.

"It's okay, baby. We have Davina and she can't hurt you."

I held on to him letting the tears fall as chaos continued outside the broken door.

The old joke that doctors make the worst patients also includes psychiatrists.

Even after the hell of tonight I was still irritated by the drafty hospital gown and the poking and prodding that came with any kind of injury. I'd had my fingernails scraped for DNA and my clothes confiscated for evidence and drywall shards picked out of my hair. Anything that would document the crime scene and keep Davina locked up was collected from my body.

I knew they were just doing their job but it didn't change the fact that I just wanted to go home and curl up in my own bed for a decade and sleep.

But even my home was a crime scene.

Ryker had shown up with a bag of clothes and things from the office and a thunderous expression on his face. I'd heard him yelling down the hallway for anyone who would listen. And then I'd heard the unmistakable sound of him telling Aiden to fuck off and the head nurse ordering them both to shut up or leave the premises.

A nurse pulled my curtain and entered the space,

checking my vitals with confident efficiency. "There are two circling pit bulls out there who are about two seconds away from getting kicked out of here. Do they belong to you?"

I sighed. "One of them is my best friend. The other is . . . was . . ." I tried to think of a way to describe what Aiden was to me but I came up blank. "The other one doesn't belong to me."

"Well I don't think he got the message." She fussed over my blankets and my IV and then gave me a level look. "Do you want them to come in? Or just one? Up to you honey."

I sighed and winced at the pain that shot through my body with the movement. I was sore all over and I knew it would get worse before it got better. I also knew that I needed to see Aiden and deal with our unfinished business.

"Send in the grumpy one with the bad attitude," I said, chuckling when she gave me a look that said she needed a little more info to know which one I was talking about. "The grumpy one with the bad attitude and the badge."

She looked surprised at my choice but I didn't have time to process it before she'd exited the area and told Aiden I wanted to see him. Through the slit in the curtain I could see him level a shitty, "I won" look at Ryker who flipped him the bird before Aiden moved towards me with purpose. The nurse stopped him with an arm bar across the chest and a withering stare.

"If you cause any more problems in here, hotshot, I'll kick you out of my ER. I don't care what kind of badge you've got on. Am I clear?"

Aiden's expression was subdued with a hit of embarrassment. 'Yes ma'am."

"You don't fool me with that ma'am business. I meant what I said," she warned him and then exited the area, pulling the curtain closed to give us some semblance of privacy.

Aiden laser focused on me and headed straight for the

bed, his hands outstretched but I scooted back on the pillows, shaking my head.

"Don't touch me," I said, wincing at the harshness in my voice and the matching hurt on his face. "I just can't. I'm so thankful you were there but I can't have your hands on me. It's too hard."

"I thought . . ." Aiden began, his hands clenched at his sides as he swallowed hard, struggling to control his emotions and his reaction to my words. "I thought we . . ."

"You thought that showing up at my place and saving my life was going to make everything okay? I'm so thankful that you were there but it doesn't change anything that went down between us. You said what you said and my gratitude won't change it."

"What I said was shitty and awful. I'm so sorry."

I examined his face, his body language and I knew he was telling the truth. He wasn't a bad man. He just wasn't the man for me.

"Yeah, I know. But you didn't say that it wasn't true." He opened his mouth to argue with me but I cut him off.

"Aiden, I'm not naïve enough to know that being with me is easy. My lifestyle isn't mainstream and it can appeal to people at first glance. It looks exciting and daring and decadent and everyone thinks they can roll with it. You're not the first person who thought they could share me and couldn't when the reality and not the fantasy porn video showed up on the sidewalk outside of my apartment."

"I know I shouldn't have been there," he said, running a hand over the scruff on his chin as he tried to explain away the night that had blown us apart before we'd really had a chance. "I was at work and this guy, another officer, said shit about you and we got into it."

He gestured to the swollen lip and the bruise on his

cheek. I could picture the scene in my mind as clearly as if I'd been standing there and witnessed it real time.

"So, what did he do? Call me a whore? Porn star? Did he ask if you minded having a girlfriend who spread her legs for everyone?" The stricken expressions and tight-lipped grimace told me I'd hit the mark. "Did he question what kind of man you were to let your woman fuck other people?"

"I wasn't going to stand by and let him talk about you like that," he argued, his voice stubborn and spoiling for another fight. I wasn't going to give him one.

"I'm a big girl and I stopped defending my life choice a long time ago so don't make this about me Aiden. That fight and the scene you caused at my home was all about you and your ego."

"You make me sound like a dick."

I shook my head, he was still missing the point. "No. You acted like one last night but you're a good man. But you're not the guy who can accept me and everything about me. It doesn't make you a bad guy and it doesn't make me defective. We're just incompatible." I smiled but it was tight and I resisted the urge to rub my chest where it ached. I'd been way more invested in this man than I'd previously allowed myself to realize and this was hard. Painful. I'd get over it but it wasn't going to be quick and it wasn't going to be easy. "It's no different than if you'd been an Orioles fan. Some things are just not going to work."

He stared at me, his jaw working with the tension so clearly working through his body. I waited, memorizing everything about him, knowing that this would likely be the last time I saw him. DC was a big enough town and we ran in such different circles, a casual meeting at the local Whole Foods was unlikely. As quickly as he'd landed, Detective Aiden Cross would leave my life.

"Carla, I just don't understand why you need it."

I smiled, blinking back the tears that I would blame on my injuries and the shitty night. "I know. But I'm not asking for you to understand, I'm just asking for you to accept it and love me anyway."

AIDEN

"I hate driving with the blue lights on my unmarked vehicle."

I glanced at Ryker, standing like a Centurian at the entrance to Carlas' partitioned room. His body language told me that I'd had my chance and I'd have to get through him to see her again. In fact, he looked like he's love to kick my ass and make sure I ended up as a guest in this place very soon. I was glad that Carla had someone like him in her life. If only to protect her from guys like me.

"Why do you think I give a shit?" He asked, his voice pitched low but fill with animosity. I ignored his taunt and continued with what I needed to say.

"I hated it when I was a beat cop. I couldn't fucking wait to get an unmarked and not have them mounted on top of the car."

I crossed my arms over my chest, leaning against the wall opposite her room watching the medical staff buzz around other patients and the cops working tonight's incident. Davina was down the hall, sedated and ready for transport back the facility she'd escaped from and where she'd probably be spending the rest of her life. I closed my eyes, once again picturing the blood all over the floor, across Carla's couch and walls. I rubbed at my chest, reliving the pain that had slammed through me when I'd gotten to her apartment.

"I got a call from a buddy on dispatch tonight and he told me that there was a report of shots fired at Carla's address. I didn't even think about it, I turned on those goddam lights and broke every law on the books to get to her place. I didn't know what I'd find when I got there but when I saw the blood . . ."

"So, you think that playing the 'white knight' is going to make up for what you did?"

I shook my head. "You heard her in there. It's too late for that. I made her feel cheap and ugly and I blew it."

He didn't deny that he'd been eavesdropping but I didn't expect him to. I'd have done the same thing. I glanced at my watch, I had to be on shift soon and really there was no reason for me to stay. Carla had dismissed me like a Queen from her bed when the dragon lady nurse had come in to give her some meds. Once word from Carla and her designated protector had put me out like yesterday's garbage.

But I stood here in the hall unable to leave and having no reason to stay.

"I don't think you're a dick, man," Ryker said from his post, his expression blank. "You treated her well, you made her laugh and she liked you. She felt comfortable with you and that takes a lot."

"That doesn't help me now," I grumbled, indulging in a pity party for one.

"Now, you're acting like a pussy."

I whipped my head up and glared at him. "What the fuck is your problem, Ryker?"

"Jesus, can you make this not about you for five seconds? Because until you do, you're never going to get a second chance with her" He glared at me, silently asking if I was going to listen or not. When I nodded he continued, his tone resigned but not unfriendly. "Think about what kind of woman Carla is. She works with at-risk kids who nobody wants to help and who all need a second chance and a little help." He pointed to his chest, his tattooed arm flexing with the tension he held tightly coiled in his body. "She took in an ex-convict who went up for killing somebody and gave him a chance when even the local grocery store wouldn't hire him. She spends her days helping people who have nowhere left to go and no one to listen. She doesn't judge and sure as hell doesn't make people feel like shit for the choices they've made. She sticks by you, quietly offering support and unconditional love."

I saw where he was going with this and I could feel the shame creeping across my skin like a brand that would burrow into my soul. I'd never get rid of it until I made this right.

Ryker wasn't done. "All she asks is for one goddam person to accept her for who she is and save the judgment. One person to love her the way she loves everyone else." He pushed off the wall where he was leaning and pulled a pack of cigarettes out of his pocket, tapping the box on his hand. "If you can't do that, it's cool. But if you can, she's not going to believe some grand gesture or splashy apology. If you want a second chance, you've got to show her you've got staying power, that you won't cut and run the minute things get rough."

He walked away, his large, tattooed form disappearing into the crowd of the busy ER. Both women and men took one look at him and made a snap judgment, giving him a wide berth and a visible sigh of relief when he passed them by with no incident. They were afraid of him but Carla had looked deeper and seen the man underneath who could be a loyal friend.

She'd seen athletes and responsible young men and women in a bunch of at-risk kids at the Center.

And I'd seen what an amazing woman she was and I

couldn't get past how she didn't fix in a box I'd constructed out of my own prejudice and judgment. She'd never asked me to change, only to meet her halfway with honesty and an open-mind.

I'd worried more about what other people thought than what I knew was between us.

She just wanted someone to accept her the way she was and love her anyway.

I'd fucked up my shot to show her that it might be me.

Chapter Eighteen

CARLA

Two weeks later.

The last place I wanted to be was in the Homicide Division of the DC Police Department.

I was back at work and back at the Center, trying to get my life back to normal after the havoc created by Davina and Nathan Marsden. My bruises and cuts were healed and I'd even accepted an invitation to join one of my couples at the club later in the week. Life had gone on as I'd known it would.

But I'd be lying if I said I hadn't missed Aiden. I did. I missed his laugh and his intensity and I'd missed the joy that had filled my life when I'd been in the midst of learning more about him. He'd been interesting and fun and our time together had been filled with allure of possibility.

I'd invested more in him than I'd planned and more than I'd really known until he was gone.

I didn't hate him or hold any ill-will towards him, even though Ryker wanted to shoot him and dump him in the Anacostia for "breaking your heart and being a cowardly shit-head". Aiden had tried but my lifestyle didn't fit with how he wanted to live his life and how he wanted to love a woman. We'd had no contact for the last two weeks and I'd finally gotten to where I'd only thought about him every other hour. Progress.

So, I wasn't looking forward to seeing him and having all of my feelings reawakened. But if I wanted my stuff back, I needed to go sign a receipt and retrieve it from the officer's in the evidence department. I couldn't even bribe Ryker to go for me. Bastard.

When I stepped off the elevator I was hit with the usual buzz and noise present in a busy police station. Men and women moved all over and phones rang constantly and no one paid any attention to me.

I scanned the area until I saw the large frame of Aiden's partner, Peter. As if he read my mind, he looked over and smiled, his broad grin prompting my own. It faltered when Aiden looked up from where he sat at the adjacent desk doing paperwork, his expression guarded. I couldn't look away, I'd missed his gorgeous face so much that I stared, blatantly soaking him in until someone jostled me from behind and snapped me out of my hormone-induced-trance.

Peter made his way over to me and held out his hand in greeting, "Hey Dr. Androghetti good to see you."

"You too." I couldn't help my glance sliding over to where Aiden watched us from his desk. His stare never left my face and I felt a blush of heat and attraction creep up my neck and across my cheeks.

"I got your stuff out of the evidence room and have it all at my desk ready for you to inspect and claim," Peter said, leading me through the warren of desks with a gentle hand on my arm. "I figured you'd want to get in and out of here as quickly as possible."

"Thank you so much. I appreciate it," I said just as we

stopped at his desk, right next to Aiden. I gave him small smile, trying hard to remain cool. "Hello Aiden."

He stood abruptly, his chair scooting backward and slamming against the file cabinet behind him. The guys at the next set of desks jumped, flashing him irritated glances. He ignored them, his cheeks ruddy with either embarrassment or the rush of awareness that was pulsing between us.

"Carla. Are you okay?" He looked me over, his hand reaching out towards me but stopping just shy of touching. "I heard you went back to work already."

I nodded. "Yes. I went back full-time this week. My patients were very understanding."

"Good," he said, jamming in hands in his pockets. He was nervous and the gesture made me smile a little inside. I was glad I wasn't the only one. "That's good."

"I hate to interrupt this fascinating conversation but here's your stuff," Peter said, holding out a clear bag full of my personal items.

With a surreptitious glance at my former lover, I opened it and began the process of removing and inspecting my stuff. There wasn't much, just some of the items I'd been wearing when Davina had tried to kill me.

A snort of laughter behind me distracted me from my task and I turned slightly, looking over my shoulder. Two men, dressed in plain clothes, sat at the desk behind us. They were smirking, giving each other shit-eating glances that carried echoes of middle school boys telling fart jokes at the lunch table. I ignored them and went back to my task.

A few moments later I heard them, snide murmurs in the noise of the room.

"Surprised she found time to get off her back to come into the station."

"She only services the millions on her off-time."

I stiffened my back and prepared to ignore them. I'd

heard similar and worse before and I didn't really give a shit about what these guys thought about me. I'd never see them again. It wasn't worth it.

Aiden thought it was.

"Hunt." His voice was steady and clear and very loud. He didn't shout but the tenor of it ceased most of the conversation in the immediate area. I turned my head to look at him but he didn't notice me. "Hunt. You need to apologize to Dr. Androghetti."

"Aiden, don't . . ." I turned to fully face the scene playing out before me, reaching out to stop him from doing this. He took my hand but he didn't acknowledge my request.

"Hunt. Apologize or I'm going to finish what I started the other night."

I was puzzled for a moment but then I remembered. His bruised cheek and knuckles. The fight at the station with another officer. This was the guy.

"Aiden, please don't."

He looked at me, his expression raw as he tightened his hold on my hand. "No. Carla. He needs to apologize." And then he turned back to the others, continuing his demands. "This woman has done nothing to deserve what you just said. She helps people and kids who have problems. She's a Nationals superfan and was a championship-level rower in college. She's kind and honest about who she is and she lives that truth every day. What she does in bed and who she does it with has nothing to do with you or any of us. She's just a person, trying to live her life." He paused, looking and me and giving me a half-smile that lit up his eyes and made everyone else disappear for the moment before he returned his attention to the men behind us. When he continued, his voice had lost all touches of tenderness and was replaced with menace and steel. "So, just apologize and I promise that I won't beat the shit out of you later.

It was the most gorgeous thing I'd ever heard and my heart did an aerial flip-flop in my chest. I blinked back tears, willing myself to not lose my shit.

The silence deepened around us as people waited to see what would happen next. When the apology came, it was like a balloon deflated and sucked all the air out of the room.

"I'm sorry," Hunt mumbled, his eyes downcast and his movements jerky. When his partner added his own to the mix, I exhaled. Aiden squeezed my hand and let it go, sliding back in his seat to continue his work. He didn't look at me and the hurt that grabbed me in the gut took my breath for a moment. He'd been kind, my knight in shining armor. He had pledged to serve and protect after all. That's all it was.

"It's fine." I swiveled and turned back to the task at hand, quickly going through my things and signing the receipt. I handed the paper over to Peter and shook his hand, turning to Aiden at the last possible second. He transferred his attention from his computer to my face, his smile friendly but distant. "Thank you, Aiden."

"You're welcome."

I hesitated for a moment but there was nothing left to say.

Except Goodbye.

———

AIDEN

I watched her leave from the corner of my eye.

Peter settled in across the desk from me with a heavy sigh that I ignored. That had gone better than I'd expected even with Hunt acting like a dick. Hopefully Carla thought a little better of me now. It was the most I could hope for.

Peter sighed and I knew he wasn't going to let it go. I raised my head and found him staring at me.

"If you don't get off your ass and go get that woman, I'm going to shoot you."

I debated arguing with him until he reached for his firearm. I grabbed my jacket and threw it on as I headed for the elevator.

"Tell the Captain I had to drop a leave chit. Personal emergency."

"Hey man, Carla is headed back in from the main office. You gonna wait?"

I turned from where I stood gazing out across the Anacostia River and found Tyrique standing behind me, wearing his rowing gear and an old Georgetown rowing hoodie that had obviously belonged to Carla at one time. He stood aloof but casual, keeping his distance from me with suspicion in his eyes. I doubted that Carla had told the kids anything about what had happened between us but Tyrique had figured out that I was the bad guy.

Fair enough.

"Uh yeah," I drawled out, trying to keep my voice calm even though my damn heart was pounding against my chest wall so hard that it hurt. It had pretty much been in a permanent cycle of aching ever since I'd left her at the hospital and I knew that if I didn't fix this between us, it would be my permanent state. "I need to talk to her."

Tyrique crossed his arms across his chest, his glare piercing. "Dude are you ever here when you're not trying to apologize for fucking up?"

I began to correct his language, as I knew Carla would if she were here, but it didn't matter. What mattered is that he'd called me on it like a man protecting his friend and mentor and I would meet him in that place.

"So far . . . that would be no. I seem to always fuck it up with her these days."

Tyrique was mad at me, his mouth now screwed up in a grimace and his eyes narrowed to slits of frustration. I braced myself for impact.

"Well. This is how I see it. Carla is the best friend I've ever had and she takes care of all of us at the center when kids at school and our parents don't get that being queer isn't a choice that they can beat or mock out of us. She'd stood up to the biggest dudes and made them back down and act right and she's helped us all be cool with who we are. So, when I see her all upset and crying and sad because you fucked up again, I gotta tell you that I got no patience with you."

"I respect that, man," I began but he cut me off.

"I'm not done," he said, moving closer to point straight at me. "You made her laugh and we were all glad to see it and if you can do that from now on, we'll be happy for her. But if all you're gonna do is make her sad then I hope she comes in here looking like your favorite fucking wet dream and grinds you under the heel of her $800 shoes and that's the truth."

"Tyrique, you need to watch your language," Carla said from behind us and we both turned to stare at her. He looked sheepish for a moment, dipping his head in acknowledgement of her admonishment.

"Sorry, Carla," he said, but then he lifted his chin with conviction and met her gaze head-on. "But I stand by what I said. You're too good to all of us and you deserve better. You deserve to be happy."

"I agree," I said, stepping closer to her. She'd changed from the station and was now dressed in her workout gear, her long hair pulled back into a high ponytail that swayed when she moved and the lemon scent of her shampoo washed over me. I'd loved waking with that fragrance all over me, wrapping me up in everything that was Carla. "And I'd like the chance to talk to you about it."

She considered me for a long moment. Her dark eyes unreadable as she considered my request. I had no doubt that my getting the chance to talk to her was not guaranteed. Carla was angry and had every right to be.

"Carla, please. Just give me five minutes."

Long moments passed before she turned to Tyrique. "Jamie is up at the office and he'll give you a ride back to the Center, okay?"

He nodded, everything about his body language communicating just how much he didn't want to leave her here with me but he agreed with a terse nod of his head and a warning glance in my direction. I nodded back at him, trying to convey my promise to try my best to make this right.

Once we were alone, the air grew thick, as if a sudden blanket of humidity had cloaked the area and made it almost impossible to breathe. I had to fight the urge to grab her and haul her up against me. The attraction was still there, the pull of desire and elemental need and I knew that if I kissed her, held her, made her come and shake and moan then we'd work out some kind of makeshift life raft designed to keep us from drowning.

But it wouldn't be what we could have had and I knew it. And goddam it, it wasn't enough Not with her. With Carla it would have to be the messy, uncharted and dangerous thing that sprang to life between us almost as soon we met.

I wanted that like I wanted my next breath.

I shoved my hands in the pockets of my jeans, the only way to keep from touching her. "I'm sorry about what happened at the station today."

"I'm fine. It's almost like it never happened."

Her words were intentional, their clear meaning punctuated by the direct stare aimed at me. She'd been open at the station until I'd shut down, protecting myself, but now she had the walls up. She was going to move on, put us behind her and I was on notice. As usual I could count on Carla to lay it all out there. It was up to me take up the gauntlet and decide whether to fight the fight or go home.

I wasn't going home without Carla. The only way to make sure that it happened was to be honest.

"I'm sorry. I was wrong." I cleared my throat, searching for the right words to say. "About everything."

She looked surprised, as if she'd been expecting anything but a straight-up, no excuses apology.

"Look, I'm just going to cut to the chase with this because if the truth doesn't get you to give me a second chance then nothing will. I was an asshole. You told me from the beginning about your kink, you were completely honest and I got angry when I actually had to deal with the truth. That's all on me."

Carla huffed out a long breath, her eyes glassy with moisture but she kept her gaze steadily on me. I had her full attention and it was more than I deserved.

"I can't lie. I had a full-on epiphany moment when I got to your apartment and you were covered in blood and huddled on the floor of bathroom. I was fucking terrified that I was going to get there too late and you were going to be dead. I realized at that moment that nothing was worse than that possibility. Not you with other men. Not you with other women. Not knowing that others get to touch you like I do." I took a deep breath but I was getting to the hardest part and I knew it could be a deal breaker for Carla. "I was afraid to lose you but I still didn't understand you. I didn't really get what made you tick so when you pushed me away, I went. I gave it up and decided to walk away. I was still an arrogant son-of-a-bitch about the whole thing. I was convinced that you were still the one who needed to change, who needed to compromise everything you are and I refused to accept all of you."

"So why are you here now? Why are we even having this conversation Aiden?" Her voice was laced with frustration and impatience and I silently pleaded for her to hear me out to the bitter end. "I don't know why you just didn't let it end at the hospital."

"Because Carla, you taught me that there is no shame in sex. No shame in who you choose to have it with or what you choose to do with them. There's only pain and jealousy in dishonesty and I was the most dishonest of all. Never you. I was the coward and the liar and one who betrayed every bit of the trust you gave me."

I had a hole in my gut that wouldn't stop hurting and I knew that the only way to fix it was to get Carla back in my life. Any way I could get her.

"So, here's my truth: I want you. In my life. In my bed. In my arms. You're already in my heart." I grabbed her face in my hands, looking down on her and praying that she understood what I was saying. "You are *the only one* I want."

She lifted her hands and circled my wrists and pulled me away, blinking back tears as she shook her head. "But I'm still a third, Aiden. I can't, won't, give it up. It's a part of me."

"And I want all of you. Everything. I don't understand why you need it but I know you do and I want you to be happy and get what you want. Making you happy is all that matters to me because someone was brave and honest and real as you deserves to have all the happiness in the world." I cupped her face again, needing to know that she heard me. "I can't promise to never be jealous but I can promise to be honest just like you've always been honest with me. I will be brave like you and I will trust that no matter what happens, you want me to be happy too. I just know that I'm not ready to lose you. Not now and maybe not ever."

"Are you sure?" She asked, her voice trembling with the unshed tears in her eyes. I used my thumbs to gather the moisture. If she cried it would kill me on the spot.

"I'm sure. Just give me a chance, okay?"

She nodded. "Okay."

"Yeah?" She nodded again. "Fuck yeah."

I kissed her over and over again, gathering her close to me and holding her tight. It was hot and sweet but I needed more. I'd missed her. God, I'd missed her so fucking much.

"There's a home game tonight if you want it come over."

She bit her bottom lip, a tease as she contemplated her options. "Will you be serving hot dogs?"

"I think I'll spring for hamburgers too," I shrugged. "It's a special occasion."

She laughed and nodded her agreement. "I'll bring the beer."

EPILOGUE

CARLA

3 months later.

"Baby, can you bring the steaks out here now? Grill's ready."

I looked out the large back of windows in Aiden's apartment, taking a moment to observe the sexy man slaving over the heated grill. Tall and lean, muscles rippling under his long-sleeved Henley, his hair sweeping over his collar. He needed a haircut and I knew that if I reminded him now and every day, he'd actually get one in about a week. He and Peter had a case, an ugly one. One that kept him out late and then had him pacing the floor at night when he did make it home.

A child's murder would never be easy but it was a nightmare for my man.

Lately he'd come to my place at the end of his long days. Tired and raw from despair and almost to the point of losing hope, he'd crawled into my bed and found refuge in my body and my home. We'd grown closer, more of a couple with each passing night.

And this morning they'd caught the monster and Aiden had called. I had come, cancelling the plans I had at Club D to celebrate this victory with me. Livvy and Rush were disappointed but they understood.

It was a delicate balance we'd struck between us. Not fragile, just precise and transparent. It wouldn't work any other way.

I still had my couples, still fed my kink and my soul with friends at Club D. I had set evenings and I was reluctant to take on new partners. Not because Aiden had asked me to cut back on new play partners, but because he hadn't. The only thing new I wanted in my life right now was him. His touch, his kiss, his affection.

His love too, maybe.

Those words had not been spoken between us yet but they were there in every night spent with each other, every laugh shared, every time he called me first when he'd faced the worst.

Love was there when he knew I was with others at Club D. It was there when he didn't ask and didn't make demands. It was there when he let me go.

And it was there when we stayed up late talking through jealousy and pain and decisions to keep this thing between us.

I would tell him. Soon.

I walked over to the door way, watching him fiddle with the grill, cursing under his breath at whatever the appliance was doing to piss him off. I smiled.

"Hey Aiden," I undid the buttons on my dress, opening it so that it could slide down my body and to the floor. He looked up, distracted at first and then his eyes landed on me, raking my body up and down. His gaze lingered on the thong as I knew it would. It was one of his favorites. "How hungry are you?"

He considered me for a moment and then he smiled. The

wicked wolf grin that was just for me. He turned to the grill and switched it off, reaching over his shoulder to gather the fabric of his shirt and whip it over his head. He was on me in three strides, his naked chest hard and warm under my hands.

His kiss was gentle but thorough, an exploration of my mouth. The complete opposite of his bruising grip on my hips. I'd have a mark tomorrow and the thought made me shiver with anticipation. We both groaned when he ended the kiss and his voice was rough with gravel when he spoke.

"Let's go work up an appetite."

READ THE FIRST BOOK IN THE SERIES

Did you love THIRD?

Read the book that started the DC After Dark
series . . . RUSH.

Atticus Rush doesn't really like people. Years in Special Ops
and law enforcement showed him the worst of humanity,
making his mountain hideaway the ideal place to live. But
when his colleagues at MacKenzie Security need him to save
the kidnapped young daughter of a U.S. Senator, he'll do it,
even if it means working with the woman who broke his heart
his ex-wife.

Lady Olivia Rutledge-Cairn likes to steal things. Raised with a
silver spoon and the glass slipper she spent years cultivating a
cadre of acquaintances in the highest places. She parlayed her
natural gift for theft into a career of locating and illegally

retrieving hard-to-find items of value for the ridiculously wealthy. Rush was the one man who tempted her to change her waysuntil he caught her and threatened to turn her in.

MacKenzie Security has vowed to save the girl. Olivia can find anything or anyone. Rush can get anyone out. As the clock winds down on the girl's life, can they fight the past, a ruthless madman and their explosive passion to get the job done?

BUY IT HERE

Dear Reader —

Thanks so much for reading my book. If you enjoyed reading about Carla and Aiden you can find out latest info on my next release and enter for the monthly giveaway by signing up for my newsletter:

NEWSLETTER SIGNUP: http://bit.ly/1hde9GD

And if you are so inclined, please leave a review on Amazon, Barnes & Noble, iBooks, or Goodreads.

I love to explore the theme of fooling around and falling in love in my books and I adore a hero who falls hard. When I'm not writing sexy, sizzling romance, I collect tasty man candy pics, indulge in a little comic book geek love, collect red nail polish, and obsess over Chris Evans. Drop me a line at robin@robincovingtonrmance.com and tell me what you obsess over!

Xx,
 Robin

Social Media Links:

Email: robin@robincovingtonromance.com
Website: http://bit.ly/1lewhMg
Facebook Profile: http://on.fb.me/YSW9n3
Facebook Page: http://on.fb.me/1fCyWuQ
Twitter: @RobinCovington
Tumblr: http://robincovingtonromance.tumblr.com
Instagram: https://instagram.com/robincovington/
Pinterest: http://bit.ly/1c1Tm5u
Amazon Follow: http://amzn.to/1L2PrAG
Street Team: http://on.fb.me/1hZdeEu
Newsletter sign up: http://bit.ly/1hde9GD

If you enjoyed THIRD, check out my other books:

A NIGHT OF SOUTHERN COMFORT
HIS SOUTHERN TEMPTATION
SWEET SOUTHERN BETRAYAL
SOUTHERN NIGHTS AND SECRETS
PLAYING THE PART
SEX & THE SINGLE VAMP
PLAYING WITH THE DRUMMER
DARING THE PLAYER
TEMPTATION
SALVATION
REDEMPTION
THE PRINCE'S RUNAWAY LOVER
ONE LITTLE KISS
SECRET SANTA BABY
RUSH
SHADOW RANCH
WHEN YOU OPEN YOUR EYES
SLEEPING WITH THE ENEMY
SEXY SECOND CHANCES

CPSIA information can be obtained
at www.ICGtesting.com
Printed in the USA
FSHW022033240920
74122FS

9 780990 543299